BOOK OF THE DEAD

SCHOLASTIC

Scholastic Children's Books
An imprint of Scholastic Ltd
Euston House, 24 Eversholt Street, London, NW1 1DB, UK
Registered office: Westfield Road, Southam, Warwickshire, CV47 0RA
SCHOLASTIC, TOMBQUEST and associated logos are
trademarks and/or registered trademarks of Scholastic Inc.

First published in the US by Scholastic Inc., 2015
First published in the UK by Scholastic Ltd, 2015

ISBN 978 1407 15700 9

A CIP catalogue record for this book
is available from the British Library.

Printed by CPI Group (UK) Ltd, Croydon, CR0 4YY
Papers used by Scholastic Children's Books are made
from wood grown in sustainable forests.

3 5 7 9 10 8 6 4 2

www.scholastic.co.uk

For S.S.G., eventually.
– M.N.

PROLOGUE

Deep in the Egyptian night, the crypt was once again alive with activity.

Black candles cast an orange glow on the sandstone walls of the burial chamber, where row after row of ancient images and carved hieroglyphs detailed a history of trickery and triumph. A mix of beetle shells and bird feathers smouldered in a bronze pot. Animal hair and shed snakeskins burned slowly in another. A harsh, burnt smell filled the air. It was the stuff of life giving off the stink of death.

For thousands of years, the same secret organization had gathered here. It was where powerful people went to avoid detection, to discuss – or to do – the unthinkable.

The members of this secret society assembled around a massive stone sarcophagus. The ancient corpse entombed within was their founder. Everything they did was to serve him. Everything they did was to bring him back.

One by one, they began a low chant in his honour.

The first to start wore a dirty grey robe. It hung heavily on his angular frame, as if weighed down by grease. On his head was a mask in the shape of a fly's head. Two large eyes bulged out from the sides and glistened in the candlelight. His voice was jittery and uneven.

The next to pick up the ominous chant wore a flowing blue-green robe. His mask was the heavy iron image of a crocodile. Together, the robe and mask showed the powerful predator emerging from its hiding place beneath the Nile.

The next chanter was so thin under her crimson robe that she might have only been a skeleton. Her voice was dry and scratchy. On her face was the pale image of a lioness, carved from bleached bone.

The last to join in was a towering figure, a good foot taller than the others. His robe was as black as a starless sky and his mask was the stuff of nightmares. An Egyptian vulture: Part scavenger, part predator, it was a creature that dealt in death and wasn't picky about the details. The beak turned from gold to iron as it hooked down to a brutal, deadly point.

The vulture's voice was strong, clear – and utterly without emotion.

As the chanting reached a crescendo, the faintest traces of other voices chorused in. Raspy whispers played on a light breeze that had no place in the sealed underground chamber.

The four stopped chanting abruptly. The phantom voices hung on half a beat longer, then faded back into the shadows.

The meeting began. They didn't bother with the usual topics: the grim business of disposing of a body, or the intricacies of expanding their vast wealth. There was only one topic tonight, something so legendary that it made everything else seem trivial.

"They have them," said the man in the fly mask.

"Yes," said the lioness. "They found them when we could not, in all our years of searching."

"They have *something*," said the crocodile. "How do we know it's really—"

"*I* know!" the vulture cut in. The others fell silent. "The Lost Spells have been found. Now all that's left is to get them ourselves. And use them."

The others shot quick, nervous looks at the sarcophagus. It was the lioness who spoke next. "They plan to keep them in plain sight; they have no idea how powerful they truly are," she rasped. "Only the woman knows."

"We need someone there when they arrive," said the fly.

The vulture-headed man looked around the chamber, pinning each acolyte in place with his gaze. "It has already been arranged," he said. "Al-Dab'u is there."

The leader raised his hand and closed it, and the black candles went out with an angry hiss. The lioness, the crocodile and the fly melted away in the darkness. Back to the surface, back to the desert night.

Once they were gone, the vulture stood motionless in the dark tomb. He'd sensed something in the room, practically tasted it in the air. Fear. These were his top lieutenants, carefully selected for their brutal efficiency. But now that the Spells were so close, even they were scared of what was to come.

He rested his hands on the cold stone of the sarcophagus.

They should *be afraid*, he thought.

Everything they had done until now had been practice.

But this – this was the real test.

The doorway between worlds would soon be opened. The power of the dead was within his reach.

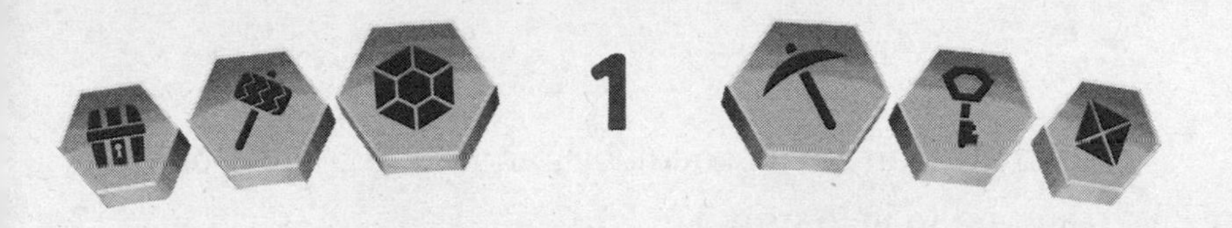

1

A DEADLY SECRET

Alex Sennefer was about to die for the first time.

He was in the Arms and Armour section of The Metropolitan Museum of Art when the pain hit. The stabbing sensation was so sharp and sudden that for a moment he thought he must have accidentally walked into one of the medieval spears. The museum had closed an hour earlier, and as he stumbled forward, the slap of his sneakers on the polished tile floors echoed through the deserted room.

He'd run out of medicine, and there was no one around to help him.

Summoning all his remaining strength, he pushed through the wing's dimly lit main hall, heading for the elevator that would take him to his mom's office. He'd felt this way before, but never this bad.

The pain that had started as a sharp stab in his centre fractured into a million pinpricks, spreading out into his limbs. Along the walls, six-hundred-year-old suits of armour watched his struggle through empty eyeholes. A troop of knights gazed down on him from replica horses, immobile, indifferent.

He shook his arms out and tried to breathe deeply, tried to relax and let the pain pass through him. Sometimes the doctors said the problem was his circulation; sometimes they said it was his digestion. But the truth? Nobody knew what was wrong with him.

With every step, he was afraid another wave of pain would come and level him. He slowly entered the American Wing and saw the elevator.

Almost there, he thought.

Breathe.

He'd been stupid not to ask his mom to order

more medicine as soon as he'd run out. But he'd thought he could bear it, and he was afraid his mom would get worried and take him to the hospital. He hated the hospital. HATED it. And his mom was seriously stressed out with work this summer. The last thing she needed was to have to worry more about him.

That seemed unavoidable now, though. He needed the spare bottle of meds that she kept for an emergency.

If he could even make it to her.

Alex reached the elevator and palm-smashed the DOWN button. After what felt like fifteen years, the elevator arrived. He fell into it. The words STAFF ONLY were printed alongside the button for floor G, but he flipped through his keys and found the little one that unlocked the elevator. He crumpled against the wall as it began to move. The cool metal felt good against his flushed face.

Alex didn't pass a single person on the way to his mom's office. It was a beautiful summer evening, and no one wanted to work late unless they had to.

I have to tell Mom, he thought. He couldn't see any way around it now. The hum of pain in his body made it hard to focus, but thoughts of the hospital flashed through his head: the tests, the needles the size of Magic Markers, and the stupid paper robes. They'd been poking and prodding him for all twelve years of his life.

There was the name tag outside his mom's office: DR MAGGIE BAUER. The door was open. The lights were on.

"Mom?" he said . . . but she wasn't there when he walked in.

Panic shot through him. The thoughts came one after another:

The museum is huge.

She could be anywhere.

I need the medicine now!

Just as he began to turn back around, he saw her purse on a chair and felt a massive surge of relief.

He tore the purse open. A wave of nausea made him squeeze his eyes shut, but he pushed his hand around inside, feeling for the smooth plastic sides of the bottle of meds she always carried for him.

Got it!

His fingers closed and he tugged the familiar orange bottle out of the purse. His stomach clenched and fluttered in anticipation. He twisted the cap off and threw two pills into his mouth – no time for water. He put the cap back on, shoved the bottle back down where he'd found it, zipped the purse, and sank to the floor, exhausted.

Breathe.

Breathe.

Breathe.

For about ten minutes, all his body could do was

Breathe.

Breathe.

Breathe.

"How long have you been here?" said his mom from the doorway.

Don't let her know.

Don't let her see me like this.

Alex pushed himself to his feet, ignoring the pain that remained.

"Couple minutes," he said, trying to sound casual. He ran his hand through his hair, using the gesture to wipe some of the sweat off his forehead.

"Are you OK?" his mom asked.

Alex shrugged.

She looked at him closely, not convinced. Alex made glancing eye contact and regretted it immediately. His mom's eyes were an intense blue grey, still penetrating and clear despite all the days she spent reading dense academic papers. Alex knew she could read him just as easily. He shifted his gaze and stared blankly at the pile of dark brown hair on the top of her head. It was pulled up and back severely. Dr Maggie Bauer had no time to worry about her hair.

"Why're you down here, hon? Do you need something?" she asked.

"Nope," he said. He tried to think of some way to change the subject. "How much longer are you going to be?"

"A while," she said. "I've got to head back to the Egyptian wing. The dead are very demanding, you know."

"Are you working on the Stung Man?" he asked, genuinely interested despite his lingering dizziness. The sarcophagus of a famous mummy known as the Stung Man was the first part of a special new exhibition his mom was curating. Alex was fascinated by it.

"No, something new," his mom answered vaguely. She usually loved to tell him all about her new projects.

"Can I come?" The Egyptian wing was Alex's favourite – not just the new show but all of it: the tightly wrapped mummies, the stone tombs, the statues of animal-headed humans and of human-headed animals, the gold and jewels and all the other treasures the ancient Egyptians thought they could bring with them to the afterlife. It was the only place in the museum where he never got bored.

His mom thought about it. "Not today," she said. "Go find Ren."

"Ren's here?" said Alex, his mood improving enormously.

"I just saw her," said Alex's mom. "I think she's on the second floor."

"OK, cool." He looked down at his feet and considered the level of pain in his body. "Oh yeah," he said. "Almost forgot. Can you order me some more medicine?"

His mom's radar clicked back on, her X-ray eyes refocused. "Did you go through it all already? Didn't we just—"

"No, no, I think I lost it." The excuse popped out of his mouth.

"You lost it?" She frowned. "You have to be careful. Just because you feel OK now. . ." He could tell she was trying to get him to realize how important the pills were without worrying him. It was a game they both played, each trying to spare the other.

He knew he should tell her what had just happened, but he couldn't. That was the other thing about her eyes: They were ringed with dark circles and surrounded by deeply etched lines. That wasn't from all the reading; that was him. His energetic, adventure-loving mom deserved a kid who could walk through the park in the summer without passing out from the heat.

Anyway, he was sure the pains would stop. They had before. He just needed a little more medicine until then.

"I know," he said. He reached up and knocked on his head, as if it were made of wood. As if he'd just done something really dumb.

But then another wave of pain pushed through the medicine and made his head swim. His mom could see the pain in his expression, he was sure, and she would realize how sick he was—

There was a knock at the door frame.

Oscar, one of the museum guards, poked his head in. His usual relaxed smile was replaced with a look of grim concern. "Hey, Dr Bauer. Mr Duran says they need you right away in the Egyptian wing. Sounds like it's pretty important."

His mom spun around. "Thanks, Oscar. Alex, you'll hang out with Ren, right?" And then she was gone.

So he wouldn't have to tell her. It would be his secret.

His own deadly secret.

2

REN

"Hey, string cheese!"

Alex had officially found Ren. She was standing in front of some angry angels in one of the European Paintings galleries. Her full name was Renata Duran, but no one called her that. Her full height was not quite four and a half feet, but it was best not to mention that, either. Her hair was dark brown and not quite shoulder length – lighter and longer than his own shaggy black hair – but her brown eyes were a mirror image of his own.

"Hey, snail trail," he replied, forcing a smile.

He was happy to see her, but the medicine had only dulled the pain, not erased it.

"I was looking for you today," said Ren. "I checked Egypt."

Alex and Ren had been best friends since for ever. They both had parents who worked at the museum, and they both went to the same school on the Upper East Side – or they had, back when Alex was healthy enough to go to real school. Now his mom homeschooled him.

"Bet I know why your mom's working late," said Ren.

"Bet I know why your dad is," said Alex. Mr Duran was a senior engineer, the go-to guy when the museum needed a new security system or display case. "The big exhibition in the Egyptian wing. It sounds like something is going on there, but my mom won't show me."

"My dad won't, either!" said Ren. "He said, like, lot of work to do, blah, blah, blah. I wonder if it has something to do with all those trips your mom took this year. Think they were for this exhibition?"

"Probably," said Alex. "She never really said, which is weird."

Ren was getting close to something that had been bothering Alex. His mother had been so mysterious about this exhibition. Usually, she told him way in advance where she was going, but some of the trips she'd made lately had been completely without warning – just a phone call in the middle of the night and the next thing Alex knew he'd be in a taxi to his aunt and uncle's place and she'd be on a flight. Usually, she brought him souvenirs from wherever she went – a snow globe from the Sahara desert, where it never snowed, or a T-shirt from a Cairo bazaar with a rock band's name spelled out in Arabic. But with these recent trips, if he got anything at all, it was something picked up in an airport – a Toblerone bar that could have been bought anywhere.

"Where were you?" he'd ask.

And every time, she found a way not to answer.

Alex thought about it some more. "Mom is really stressed out about this one. The way she sprinted over there. . . It wasn't like usual."

Ren grinned. "Want to go see what they're up to?"

"Think they'll let us?" he said.

"Think we'll ask?"

It went without saying that she meant spying. Alex considered it: the walk, the stairs. It was no small commitment for him, even on a good day, which this was not.

He glanced at Ren. She'd never push him to do something he couldn't handle, but what kind of friend couldn't even do some low-speed indoor spy work? How long until she got bored and gave up on him?

"Let's go," he said.

They crept down the stairs and went the back way to the Egyptian wing. Alex appreciated how slowly Ren walked when she was with him. He knew it defied all her instincts as a native New Yorker, but he told himself it was better for their mission. Stealth was key, after all.

They slipped quietly into the massive room housing the Temple of Dendur. As always, Alex paused a moment to take it in. It was an entire ancient temple, brought over stone by stone from the bank of the Nile River, and reconstructed next to a reflecting pool in a massive glass-walled room.

And right now, after hours, there was not a guard in sight.

They entered the maze of cool, dark rooms beyond

the temple. The display cases, their gleaming treasures lit dramatically from below or above, provided the only light. Alex and Ren slowed down and listened carefully. Their parents could be anywhere.

Alex and Ren travelled hundreds of years back in time with each doorway they passed. They made it all the way from the late eighteenth dynasty to the early twelfth before they came to a floor-to-ceiling curtain blocking off the next room. It was printed with pictures of a mummy's golden death mask and an ornate scroll. Beneath the pictures it read: CLOSED FOR RENOVATIONS: NEW EXHIBITION COMING SOON!

"Here it is," Ren whispered. "Let's see what we can find – or hear."

The prickling pain was returning to Alex's body, but he flashed Ren his best confident-spy smile. Together they slipped through the curtain. As soon as they were inside, they could hear faint voices a room or two away. Very quietly, they began looking around.

The last time they'd been in this room, it was bare, waiting for the new treasures to arrive. Now, the walls were covered with thick glass cases.

The sensation in Alex's body was amplified now. But it wasn't pain shooting through him this time.

No. It was fear.

Breathe.

Breathe.

Inside the glass cases were swaths of material – time-yellowed linen or ancient, brown-edged papyrus.

Alex only recognized a few of the hieroglyphs on the papyrus, but immediately he knew what this was. He could feel it calling to him in his bones. Crawling through his blood.

This was the Book of the Dead.

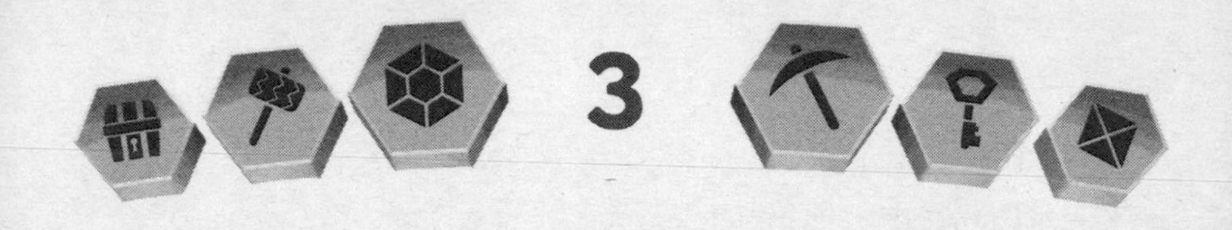

3

THE WEIGHING OF THE HEART

Breathe.

Ren could tell something was wrong.

"What?" she asked. "What is it?"

Alex got his breath back. He pushed down the fear and pain.

"It's the Book of the Dead," he told her in a low voice.

"Doesn't look like a book to me," said Ren.

She could joke, because she didn't feel the same fear that he did. He'd spent his life standing on the brink of death, and these ancient words seemed to be calling to him from the other side, pulling him forward.

"That's the modern name for it," said Alex. "Because 'Bunch of Scrolls and Scraps of the Dead' doesn't sound as good. It's like a cross between prayers and spells."

"For the dead?" said Ren.

Alex nodded. "To help them cross over into the afterlife."

Ancient Egypt was his mom's speciality, and Alex had picked up a pyramid-load about it over the years. When you think that you might die at any moment, you start to pay attention to what's written about death. And the ancient Egyptians were obsessed with the afterlife.

Steadying himself, Alex walked up to get a better look. Hieroglyphic writing in neatly printed rows covered the first third of the longest stretch of linen before giving way to a small painting.

It depicted a large set of scales surrounded by figures with animal heads – Alex immediately recognized Anubis, the jackal-headed guardian of the underworld. Everyone in the picture was looking at the scales. Alex looked at them, too. On one side was a feather, on the other. . .

He leaned in closer.

"A heart," he whispered.

There was an information plaque on the floor, waiting to be hung, and Ren knelt down to read it. "That shows the weighing of the heart," she reported. She pointed to the sole figure in the scene with a human head. "That dude just died, and he's waiting to see if his heart passes the test. If it's not weighed down by bad deeds, it will be as light as the feather, and he can enter the afterlife."

"What if it's too heavy?" Alex asked.

"Then they feed it to that thing," she said, standing up and pointing to a large, crocodile-headed creature at the bottom of the picture.

"They feed it to him?" said Alex.

Ren leaned back over and double-checked the plaque. *"Her,"* she said. "Her name is Ammit. Nickname: the Devourer."

Alex didn't have to check to know Ren was right, and not just because back in school her nickname was "Plus Ten Ren" for all the extra credit she did. He could almost feel Ammit's hot, hungry breath on his neck.

Ren peered into the case. "Look, the cloth is covered in little stains."

This time, Alex knew why. He tried to keep his tone light, but the words still chilled him.

"It's from the dead guy," he explained. "The one in the painting. A lot of times they printed the Book of the Dead right on the mummy's wrappings."

They both looked at a stain near the edge of the text: a red so dark it was almost black.

Blood.

Alex slowly backed away from the Book of the Dead towards an empty case in the middle of the room. That seemed safer. The only description was on a small tile inside the case:

EXHIBIT 7A6

"Huh," said Ren, turning and sizing up the empty case.

Alex leaned in for a closer look.

"Watch out," said Ren. She grabbed his arm with her right hand and pointed to the ceiling with her left.

Alex looked up and saw a black metal disc directly above the case, ringed with small lenses. A laser security system.

"Is it on?" he asked. This was more Ren's area of expertise, because of her dad.

She squinted up at it. "Not sure. The beams are invisible."

They looked down at the case. The high-grade acrylic glass was unusually thick. Ren's dad had told them that half an inch of the stuff was bulletproof. This was at least three times that: bombproof.

"Well, we still don't know what they're so worked up about," Alex said. "But whatever's going to go in there is getting the star treatment."

They heard voices again – coming closer.

"It's here too soon," Alex heard his mom say. "We've never dealt with something like this before – and we're not prepared to protect it."

A man answered in a low and guarded voice.

"They're in the next room," Ren whispered.

"OK, let's go," said Alex, more than ready to leave.

He usually felt at home in the museum, but there was something different about this new exhibition. There was too much death in these rooms now. Even if Ren couldn't feel it, he could.

The master spies slipped back through the curtain, leaving the room exactly as they'd found it – with one small exception.

On the Book of the Dead, something was changing.

The drop of blood they'd been looking at was 3,300 years old – but it began to glisten now.

Alive.

Again.

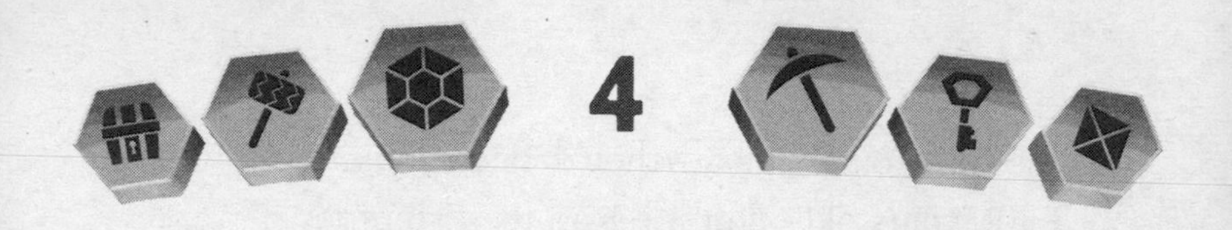

4

DEATH'S DOOR

The humidity was swamp-like as Alex and his mom waited for the crosstown bus the next morning. Everyone was sweating and impatient. Alex knew that when she was by herself, his mom walked to work. But in the last year, the trip had become too hard for him on bad days. In this heat, it was out of the question. So his mom pretended she liked the crowded, loud bus. She tried to make it an adventure, just like when she used to stay home and read to him when he couldn't make it to school, calling his sick days "story days". He could see right through it, but he played along.

When they'd gone home the night before, he'd wanted to ask her about the Book of the Dead. But he couldn't find the words to express exactly why some old rags haunted him so much.

"What's that on the horizon?" his mom said, reaching down to nudge him.

He sleepily poked his head out over Eighty-Sixth Street and peered into the distance. It always took him a long time to wake up in the morning, and today the sticky heat felt like a web he had to push through. He looked out at the traffic and finally saw what his mom was talking about. "Bus," he said.

At the sound of this single word, a pair of old men in worn-out suits roused themselves from the bus stop bench. Alex's mom leaned down and whispered, "You have powerful magic, my son. You have summoned the Ancient Ones!"

Alex managed a laugh despite his aching chest, and his mom leaned further out to check on the bus's progress. As she did, her Egyptian scarab necklace swung out and caught the morning sun. The polished blue stone shone softly and the refined copper borders gleamed. She reached out instinctively with her right hand and pressed the winged beetle back to her chest, as if pledging allegiance. It was just about the only piece of jewellery she owned, and Alex had never seen her without it.

As they climbed aboard the bus, the cranked-up air conditioning washed over them. It felt nice, but Alex stared out the window the whole way, imagining not just walking alongside the bus, but running. These daydreams never worked out for him. At recess he used to fantasize about hitting a Wiffle ball high off the wall only to end up striking out – and hurting himself on the swing. But his body felt like a prison sometimes, and daydreams were a look out the window.

The bus hit a pothole and jarred his brittle body. The dream ended. His thoughts returned to the real world.

"Is the exhibition opening today?" he asked.

His mom shook her head. "Tomorrow. There's still one last artefact we haven't installed. So we've got a ton of work to get done today to get everything ready."

Her voice was tense. Whatever this thing was, it

was important.

Soon enough, Alex and the rest of the world would discover what belonged in the case for Exhibit 7A6.

Alex looked for Ren in all the usual spots once he got to the museum. Finally, he gave up and texted her. The reply was quick and disappointing. She was on her way to the big Costco on 117th with her mom.

It figures, Alex thought. With two parents, his best friend spent half as much time at the museum as he did.

He disliked battling the crowds during the day, so he hid out in the office and played video games for hours, slipping into a trance where he could forget about his own achy body. His avatar leapt over obstacles, swung heavy objects like they were pillows, and had a special victory dance where he flexed his bulging biceps, which Alex thought was particularly impressive.

His mom came by around noon and they went to lunch at a diner. It was a short walk, but the air was hot and sticky and thick and it took Alex a long time. He'd noticed that whenever his mom had to slow herself down for him, her energy burst out in other ways. Today she fidgeted with her hair – first unclipping it from its tight bun and letting it fall down past her shoulders. Then she plucked a thick rubber band from around her wrist and put her hair up in a ponytail. His mom always had office supplies on her – literally on her. If it wasn't a rubber band on her wrist, then it would be a few paper clips fastened to her shirt pocket or a pen behind her ear. Sometimes it was all three.

The ponytail bounced as she walked, and if Alex ignored the dark circles or lines around her eyes, she looked as vibrant as any of the Manhattan go-getters around them. She'd been young when she had him: young and in Egypt. Now she was a month and a day away from turning thirty-seven. Alex had picked out her present but still needed one more week of allowance to pay for it. He wondered what her life would be like if she didn't have him to worry about. A single word slipped into his mind: *soon.*

He gave his head a quick, fierce shake, trying to dislodge the thought.

The pinpricks started up again as soon as they got back to her office. They felt stronger than usual – sharper and more electric – but he held them off by secretly taking a few more pills. As soon as Alex's mom left to head down to the exhibit, he curled up on her office couch and napped.

At the end of the day, the crowds cleared out and Alex went straight to the Egyptian wing to find his mom. He was sure that's where she'd be, but he made it through half a dozen rooms without seeing her. He decided to stay away from the Book of the Dead and moved in a different direction.

It was time to visit the Stung Man.

A large sign outside the room read:

SPECIAL PREVIEW OF THE METROPOLITAN MUSEUM OF ART'S EXCITING NEW EXHIBITION. BE QUIET, PLEASE. THE STUNG MAN IS SLEEPING – FOR ETERNITY.

The last part was new. Alex didn't blame the museum for showboating a little. People loved the story. Alex knew it by heart at this point.

The Stung Man had been a master thief, operating for years without being caught. Alex imagined that if they'd had "wanted" posters in ancient Egypt, this guy's face would have been all over them.

Eventually, the thief was pursued by the pharaoh's men into the desert, where he hid in a small cave.

Alex always imagined what that must have felt like: that brief feeling of victory, of having escaped a terrible fate.

And then. . .

The Stung Man wasn't called the Stung Man at that point, not yet. Everyone gets their nickname for a reason.

As the pharaoh's men searched outside, the thief discovered that his hiding spot was full of scorpions.

Alex tried to imagine it. Was there light in the cave, or was it the sound of skittering legs that first alerted him to the fact that something was wrong? By then it didn't matter, because they were on him. The thief was stung again and again, all over his body: his legs, his torso, his arms, his neck. His face.

He refused to call out.

He chose death over capture.

When they finally found him, he was swollen past recognition. His stubborn courage earned the pharaoh's grudging respect. The Stung Man was given a lavish burial and a story that would last for thousands of years.

Standing in front of the thief's mortal remains, Alex shuddered. He was no stranger to stinging pains himself – and he knew what it was like to bite down on your tongue so no one would hear you cry out.

The massive stone sarcophagus was decorated with dozens of images of scorpions. The pharaoh, apparently, had a twisted sense of humour. Alex walked right up to the exhibit and looked at the scorpions. They were painted with real, untarnished gold. When the light struck them, it made the scorpions appear to move.

Alex knew the sarcophagus was only the outer case, heavy enough to fend off everything from rats to grave robbers. Inside, there would be an elaborately decorated outer coffin, and then a smaller inner coffin. And inside *that* . . . the Stung Man himself, embalmed and wrapped tightly in linen.

Four canopic jars sat outside the sarcophagus, ceremonial alabaster vessels that contained the Stung Man's internal organs: the lungs, the stomach, the liver, the intestines.

Only the heart would be left inside the mummy itself. Left inside so it could be weighed and judged.

As Alex examined the jars, he got the creepy sensation of being watched. He swung his head around but saw nothing.

He shook it off and looked back at the jars. The tops were carved in the shapes of different heads: a baboon's, a jackal's, a man's, and a falcon's. "Every god has a job," his mom liked to say about ancient Egypt, and Alex knew these four were in charge of pickled people parts. He leaned in for a closer look at the falcon and immediately got that creepy feeling again, like an icy finger on the back of his neck.

"Hello, young man."

Alex jumped about three feet. When he landed, he held his breath and stood absolutely still as the adrenaline drained away.

Surprises were not good for him.

He looked at the man who'd spoken. The first thing that jumped out about him – hopped out, really – was that he looked a little like a toad. He had big protruding eyes and no chin to speak of. He was wearing a crisp black suit with a staff pass pinned to his jacket.

Alex had never seen him before.

Breathe.

"Sorry," Alex said to the man, trying to cover how shaky he felt. "You scared me."

"I'm very sorry," said the man, in a way that didn't sound sorry at all. Alex was pretty sure he recognized the accent.

"Are you German?" he asked.

"I am, in fact," said the man.

"Thought so. You sound like my grandmother. I mean, not like an old woman, but . . . yeah."

A pained look flashed across the man's face. "I am Dr Todtman, from Berlin. And who might you be?"

"I'm Alex . . . Alex Sennefer."

"Sennefer, yes," said Todtman, a hint of actual interest in his voice. "The Keeper of the Seal."

Alex was impressed that the man had pronounced his name perfectly, with the emphasis on the second syllable: sen-NEF-er. That took most people a few tries.

But as for the rest of it . . . Alex had no idea what the man was talking about.

"The what?" he said.

"Sennefer, the Keeper of the Seal," said Todtman.

"Keeper of a seal? Like at a zoo?"

"Like at a palace," said Todtman. "In the eighteenth dynasty, Sennefer was the keeper of the pharaoh's seal, an important man."

"Oh, right," said Alex. "That kind of seal."

"I thought your name would be Bauer," said the man. Alex looked at him carefully. He hadn't mentioned his mother.

"It was my dad's name," said Alex. "Is," he added quickly, and then felt stupid. He honestly didn't know.

"I'm surprised she didn't tell you," said Todtman, his expression unreadable.

"Tell me what?" Before Alex had even finished the question, he heard his mom's footsteps. He turned around and saw her stride quickly into the room. The ponytail was long gone; she was back in business mode.

"Alex, honey," she said. "We'll just be a few minutes. Why don't you go wait out by the temple?"

"But" – he tried to think of some way he'd be allowed to stay – "I was just talking to the doctor."

"I'm sure you were," said his mom. "Now off you go. We have some important work to do here."

"But. . ."

"Shoo!" She said it with a smile, but she said it nonetheless. If Alex didn't know better, he'd think she didn't want him to have anything to do with this man. He gave him one more look: black suit, froggy features and the icy eyes that Alex had felt burrowing into his back.

Stepping out of the room, he pulled out his phone and texted Ren. No response. He sat there and thought about what the man had said. Alex didn't know much about his father, except that he didn't know much about his father.

He *did* know that his father was Egyptian. And now he knew something else, something about his name. It was just a scrap of ancient trivia, he figured. Still, it was a nice addition to a very small collection.

He knew he was supposed to head out of the exhibition, back to the temple or his mom's office. But despite his earlier reluctance, something was drawing him back to the room that held the Book of the Dead.

The case for Exhibit 7A6 wasn't empty any more.

The lenses of the security system shone now with bright pinpricks of red light. The lasers were on. If anyone broke one of the beams, the whole room would turn into the Fourth of July: flashing lights and blaring sirens.

Carefully, Alex leaned in.

It was a linen scroll covered in gold hieroglyphs.

Alex had seen a lot of scrolls, but never one like this. Out of the corner of his eye, he saw a sign next to the case. He wanted to read it, but for some reason he couldn't stop staring at the strange scroll.

Finally, he peeled his eyes away and read three words he couldn't believe.

THE LOST SPELLS

He almost wanted to laugh. That was impossible. The Lost Spells were just a legend.

"They're not real," he whispered, even though there was no one around to hear him.

But they *were* real. He was looking at them. In fact, he still couldn't stop. His eyes were beginning to burn.

He finally managed to blink – and reality rushed back in. His body was betraying him again. There was the weakness and fatigue, the pinpricks in his chest and the tingling in his limbs. There was the sense of fragility, as if he were living his life on a narrow ledge a hundred feet above the street. But there was something else now, too. His head was buzzing, and when he closed his eyes again, all he saw was a jumble of golden symbols.

I have to get out of here.

He shook his head, trying to clear it, and stumbled into one of the Old Kingdom rooms but couldn't go any further. Just past the entrance there was a small tomb, and Alex leaned heavily on the ancient stone. Next to him was a false door – a vertical strip in the rock, like a narrow passage, with inscriptions on either side.

It was a gateway for the spirit to travel between the world of the living and the world of the dead.

The buzzing in Alex's head was louder now. The surface of the false door seemed to flicker and shift. He tried to keep going, but once again his view of the stone seemed to bend and warp, as if he were looking at shimmering pavement on a hundred-degree day.

He felt a sudden sharp pain in his stomach. Without looking away, he reached into his pocket and pulled out his medicine. But before he could unscrew the cap, he saw something new.

Shadows edged the false door in the stone, and for just a second he saw those shadows take shape. The head of an animal turned to face him, a long dark snout and two eyes that glittered red like rubies. A fresh wave of pain shot through him. He fumbled with the safety cap on the bottle. It popped off just as a stronger jolt rocked him.

Alex felt like he'd been stabbed with a power cable. He collapsed and a shower of white pills went everywhere, skittering across the floor and into the corners.

There was a long silence.

The pain was duller now, far away. Alex could feel the shadows coming, covering his body, crowding towards his heart.

Then there were footsteps. Distantly, he could hear a scream. Distantly, he could hear people come running. The marble floor felt cold against his cheek and his nostrils filled with the faint, vinegary smell of tile cleaner. He watched as shoes crushed the precious pills into powder. He wanted to say something, but the pain had travelled up into his chest now, and the only sound he could make was a low gurgle.

A guard was there.

Then his mother was there.

Alex tried to say something to her. He wanted to apologize, though he couldn't remember exactly what for. He let his eyes close. There was the open door – and on the other side, the jackal's eyes gleaming in the dark.

"We're losing him," someone said. "We're losing him."

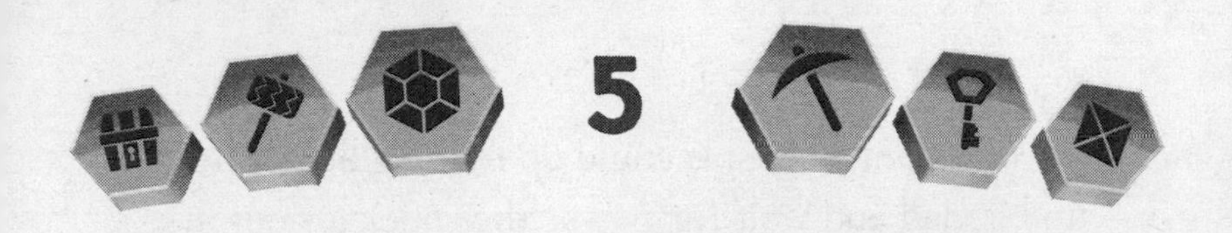

5

BORROWED TIME

They were not letting Ren in to see Alex, and she was not cool with that. She looked around the waiting room, which was full of people in varying degrees of misery. Ren diagnosed a few. There was a middle-aged woman with a hacking cough; an old man with a head wound, still bleeding; a little kid with an ice pack on his knee: probably sprained.

Lucky, she thought. *At least they know what's wrong with them. At least they're in a place that can fix it.* Meanwhile, she could do nothing but sit next to her dad and wait for news. She snuck a sideways look at him. He was wearing a blue button-down shirt, the sleeves rolled up past his elbows for a workday that was long over. She tried to read his expression, but the angle was weird.

"How bad is it, do you think?" she asked. "When will they let us in to see him?"

"I don't know, Ren-Ren," he said. She didn't know if he was answering the first question, the second question, or both.

There was a TV mounted on the wall in the corner of the room, playing a news channel without the sound. She watched it for a while. Something bad had happened in India. She saw smoke and flames and a train on its side. She looked away once she saw the first body.

"Will they call our name?" she asked. "Even though we aren't patients?"

Ren knew it was a dumb question as soon as she said it. She hated sounding dumb, especially around her dad. But this time, the guy famous at the museum for having all the answers hadn't even heard the question.

"Uh-huh," he said without bothering to look over.

He was staring intently at his phone. A scientific diagram filled the little screen. That was the other thing about him: always busy. Having all the answers took time.

"You're *working*?" Ren said loudly.

Now he looked over. "There's not much else to do, Ren-Ren. We just have to wait until he's healthy enough for visitors."

The way he said it made her feel better, like it was just a matter of time. She was still a little mad: It wasn't just the dumb things she said that he missed. But she took a deep breath and tried to let it go. This trip was not about her. "What is that, anyway?" she said, nodding towards the diagram on his phone. "The Death Star?"

"Plumbing system," said her dad. "There's some kind of problem with the new exhibition. Things are a little too . . . fresh. Think there might be too much moisture in the room."

"But the rooms are climate-controlled," she said. She listened carefully to him, even if he didn't always return the favour. "How do you think it's getting in?"

Her dad looked up from the phone and into the distance, as if picturing something. "That's a good question," he said, and Ren felt her cheeks flush. "Those rooms are right over the drainage sub-basement, though. So the plumbing could have something to do with it."

He went back to staring at his phone, and Ren went back to worrying about Alex.

"Did you mean it?" she asked her dad after a while. "What you said?" She was thinking of *"until he's healthy enough,"* but they weren't on the same page.

"Yeah," he said. "I think it's the plumbing."

Two floors up, Alex was lying on a very clean bed. He had electrodes taped to his chest, a sensor clamped to one finger, and an IV tube running into his left arm. The rest of him was tucked tightly under crisp white sheets. The adjustable bed had been raised so that his upper body was slightly higher than his feet. His eyes were closed and he wasn't moving.

That was the story of his body.

His mind was more active. It flickered and buzzed like a lightbulb about to go out for good. He wasn't quite conscious, but he occasionally rose close enough to the surface to hear something. Sometimes it was a scrap of conversation between nurses. More often, it was just the beep and hum of machines.

Under the noise of the machines – in-between the beeps, at the low ebb of the hums – was another, quieter sound. It was a steady stream of soft words, mostly too muted to make out, but he recognized the rhythms. He knew on some level that it was his mom. She was reading to him, like she had when he was little. He wanted to listen, but the more he tried to climb to the surface, the more he slipped away.

He felt himself going under.

And then, for a while at least, he felt nothing.

When he came around again, Alex could see the hospital room very clearly. The doctors were gone, and his mom was, too. An empty chair was pulled up at an angle, one arm nearly touching his bed. And there he was, tucked under the sheets with his eyes closed. The sheets had been folded back and he had a surprising number of tubes and wires attached to him.

That's when he realized that he wasn't supposed to be looking down at his own body like this. His head swam with the realization. Except he was looking at his head, so. . . He couldn't process it. He felt like he was all eyes and no brain, and just like that, he was out in the hallway.

His mom was there, too, just outside the door. He tried to say, "Mom, I'm here," but nothing came out. She was waving her arms, shouting. A moment later, a small squad of doctors and nurses came charging down the hall and ran right past him.

They all rushed into the room, and his mom went in after them. Panic broke over him like a wave. He knew what this was now. He was dying. His body – his stupid body – was finally giving up.

No wonder it all seemed so peaceful.

The fight was over.

He had lost.

But he wasn't ready for this.

He had to try. Something. Anything.

He remembered the old Egyptian legends, the ones his mom had read to him. He suddenly realized that that's what she'd been reading to him from his bedside.

Because in those stories, the soul could travel.

He had no legs or arms. All he had was what he saw. He tried to push forward with that, like he was leaning in for a better look.

Nothing happened. Panic mixed with despair.

He called out silently to his mom again. And then, slowly at first and then all at once, his vision turned and raced back through the open door. He felt the rush: equal parts exhilaration, fear, and hope. The machines were all going crazy, screaming out their beeps. He saw his body, and the circle of people around it. He tried to push past, but they were blocking him. The fear surged. He pushed again. He screamed out along with the machines.

His world went dark once more.

Maggie Bauer was standing as stiff as a board just inside the door. She wasn't really supposed to be there, but the hospital staff had more pressing concerns. Her hand was at her neck, wrapped around her scarab amulet. The room was a hive of activity, with hospital staff coming and going like frenzied bees.

"Clear!" shouted the lead doctor. The light above her dimmed briefly, and then her son took a long overdue breath – a gasp, really. Technically speaking, he'd been dead for just under two minutes.

The lead doctor tried to brush past her on his way out of the room, but she stepped in front of him and looked him in the eyes. She needed an honest answer, now. He just shook his head.

Her son was living on borrowed time, and it wouldn't last.

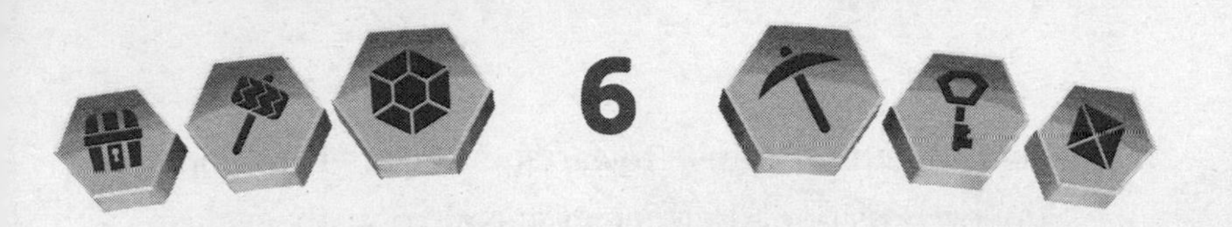

6

DARKNESS

Ren and her dad had left the hospital with no news, but at breakfast the next day, she knew she was about to get some.

"Hey, Ren-Ren, we need to talk about something," her dad said as he sat down at the table, pronouncing each word like he was being graded on it.

"It's about Alex, isn't it?"

"'Fraid so," said her dad.

Ren looked across the table and there was her mom, dressed in her standard spray of bright colours and leaning towards her in Emotional Support Position. Perfect as usual, not an eyelash out of place.

"Oh my God, is he. . ."

"No, no," said her dad, putting his hands up in a double stop sign.

Ren exhaled.

"But he had a close call over the weekend," said her dad. "Really close."

Ren looked down at her Cinnamon Toast Crunch, which was slowly turning to Cinnamon Toast Mush in the skim milk.

Her mom put her hand on her wrist, and it really bothered Ren how much she appreciated that. She looked down at the freshly painted nails on her mom's hand, and the freshly chewed ones on her own.

"His heart stopped for a while. It was a close call."

Ren absorbed the news like a body blow. Her mom squeezed her wrist, but this time she shook her off.

"His condition has stabilized, but. . ."

Ren nodded again. She read her dad's tone as much as his words. Arrows stabilize before they fall, too. Her parents' body language told her the same thing: downcast eyes, slumped shoulders. However they'd got Alex's heart started again, she knew he wouldn't make it through Round Two.

"Can I see him?" she said. It was a test as much as anything.

Her parents exchanged a quick look.

"They think that would be possible," said her mom, finally joining the conversation.

They don't expect him to make it, she thought. *But they're wrong.*

"But it won't be. . ." her mom began before pausing to fumble for the right words. Her years of public relations experience crumbled against the gritty details of life and death. "There's a breathing tube now and. . ."

Ren gave her a look: *Does it look like I care about that?*

"You promise you'll take me?"

Her dad nodded, and that was the end of the conversation. Ren got up and dumped her sugary skim-milk mush in the sink.

She spent the day at the museum. She wanted to be close to her dad, in case anything changed with Alex and they had to make a quick trip.

A last trip.

She tried to delete those words from her mind as soon as she thought them.

She went and sat in her favourite place in the museum, probably her favourite place in the world. It was on the second floor in European Paintings: a little bench in the middle of a roomful of paintings by Rembrandt.

She looked around at the familiar artworks. They were dark and mysterious, with lively eyed, ruddy-faced men and women emerging from the black and brown murk. She didn't know why she liked these particular paintings so much. The Met was full of world-famous masterpieces.

She liked that these were realistic, though. Rembrandt was a great painter, not just a great artist. She admired his competence as much as anything, how he somehow made recognizable images out of thick swoops of goopy paint. She had no patience for the painters who slapped down a few quick lines or splashes of colour and walked away. She didn't understand genius – how some things came so easy to some people – but she understood hard work. She understood that if you worked hard enough, you could get the same results as the people who didn't have to work hard at all. And she could see the work in Rembrandt's paintings. The figures were built up in layers, carefully crafted. They were realistic, just really dark. And now, for the first time, she thought maybe she understood why she liked him best.

She thought about Alex, lying in a hospital with a tube in his mouth. She thought about that night in the waiting room, watching a train wreck on TV, surrounded by the sick and injured and a dad too busy to hear her. And finally, she thought this: *Dark is realistic.*

7

FOR LATER

Tuesday morning was bright and sunny, which Ren resented. She and her dad were finally on their way across town to visit Alex in the hospital. Their taxi was stuffed full of all the cards, flowers and gifts the Met staff had given them for Alex.

The taxi was quiet and Ren searched her brain for something to say. She peered around a *Get Well Soon!* balloon to see her dad. "There was a really big line for the new exhibition," she offered.

Her dad nodded and went back to looking out

the window on the other side. He had that same far-off look on his face, puzzling out some new problem.

That was dumb, she thought. *It wasn't a question.*

She tried again. "What are they all there to see?"

He glanced over. "The Lost Spells," he said. "They're big news."

"Oh, right, those," she said. "Yeah, those are pretty important."

As soon as he looked away again, she hid behind the balloon, slipped her phone from her pocket, and typed *Lost Spells* into its web browser.

The first page of results was all from sword and sorcery games and fantasy movies. She added *Egypt* and things improved. She picked an official-looking link – from the British Museum in London – and began to read. The first part, she already mostly knew: *The Egyptian Book of the Dead has long been thought to consist of some two hundred known spells. Ancient priests used these texts to help the spirits of the dead transition smoothly into the afterlife.*

The next part was more interesting: *However, there were reputed to be nine additional spells. Though some scholars believe them to have been lost or destroyed long ago – and others insist they never existed in the first place – these so-called Lost Spells were said to be far more powerful. Some were even reputed to allow the spirits of the dead to return to their physical—*

"What're you reading over there?" her dad interrupted.

She tilted the screen away from him. "I'm on the British Museum site."

Her dad smiled. "My little Einstein."

Ren looked away. She wished he wouldn't call her that. *He* was the Einstein. *He* was the one who grew up speaking only Spanish at home and put himself through the best engineering school in the US. She had it ten times easier, and it still wasn't enough.

He had no idea how much extra work – how many extra questions – it took her just to keep up. *Plus Ten Ren* . . . she hated that, too. Alex was the only one who'd never called her that. He'd always understood, because he was trying to seem better than he really was, too.

The taxi pulled up at the hospital and they went inside. The waiting room looked a little different in the daylight, but it smelled the same. The scent of chemical cleaners tickled Ren's nostrils. Underneath the bright scent of fake lemons she could just make out the last stubborn traces of sweat, urine and decay.

Almost immediately, a nurse came out to lead them up to Alex's unit. A sign read: PAEDIATRIC INTENSIVE CARE. *Sick kids,* thought Ren. She couldn't believe how nervous she was. She wanted to see Alex, but she was dreading it, too, which made her feel like a jerk.

"This is his room," said the nurse, reaching down and pushing on the door handle. "I'll be right outside."

"Thank you," said Ren's dad before shouldering through with his armful of flowers.

Ren – who was holding the cards and gifts – didn't trust her voice, so she looked up at the nurse and nodded.

"Hi, Maggie!" called her dad in an exaggeratedly cheery voice. "Special delivery."

But Dr Bauer wasn't there. They both looked around the room. Ren looked at everything except the bed.

"That's weird," said her dad.

"She's not back at the museum, is she?" said Ren.

"No, she's on leave. Dr Todtman took over for her. She's probably just grabbing some food."

Ren found a table and unloaded all the gifts except the one from her. It was a book. She knew Alex couldn't read it now, but he had enough flowers and she knew he wouldn't want another stuffed animal.

The room was dimly lit and the blinds were closed. Ren looked at the sunlight slipping in around the edges until, finally, she was ready to look at Alex. She did it in one quick motion. *Like tearing off a bandage*, she thought, and then hated herself for it. And then there he was.

Alex had always seemed kind of large to Ren. Really, everyone seemed kind of large to Ren. But not now. Now he seemed small, swallowed up by the bed and shrink-wrapped by the sheets, except for his head, shoulders and arms. His arms had to be outside the sheets, she saw, because they had so many things going into and out of them. And then there was the mask and the hose that led from it and the machine it led to. She had known it would be there. She'd recognized the Darth Vader sound of mechanical breathing from the hallway.

Alex's face looked the same but different, as if a thin, clear layer of wax had been brushed over his tan skin. *Less animated* – those were the words

Ren settled on, because it was the nicest way to put it.

She watched him closely, looking for any signs of movement: a blink, the twitch of a finger.

Nothing.

"Hi," she said.

She thought of the thousands – maybe millions – of words they'd exchanged over the years. Sometimes talking over each other because they had so much to say. Now she couldn't think of anything else to say at all.

Fortunately, she had a few extra words already written down. She knew what everyone thought. She heard them talking about Alex as if he were already dead. Even his own mother wasn't there. Ren had no control over any of that. All she could do was make up her own mind.

As her dad bustled around the room, looking for flat surfaces and containers for the flowers, Ren slid the book across the crisp, flat sheet and under Alex's hand. It was a paperback copy of *Watership Down*. Her class had read it in school that spring, after he'd left. She hadn't liked it that much – rabbits don't talk! – but she thought he might. Inside there was a ten-dollar gift card to the bookstore. Her mom had bought the book, but Ren had bought the gift card on her own. It read, in whole:

TO: ALEX

FROM: REN

FOR LATER.

He was her best friend, and she would not give up on him.

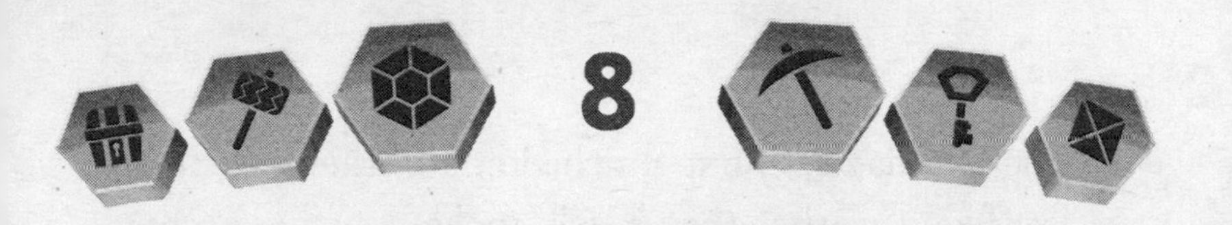

8

THE LOST SPELLS

Dr Bauer returned to the hospital a few hours later. She entered the room dressed for business, wearing a power suit and carrying a black leather briefcase. She walked across the polished floor as if she were covering the last few feet of a tightrope, her steps fast but measured, her lips pressed flat with purpose. She pulled the chair back up to Alex's bedside, put down the briefcase, and picked a battered old book up off the night table.

A nurse named Helen fluttered around the room.

The two had spent so much time together over the last few days that they barely spoke now, just went about their respective tasks. Helen swapped out an empty IV bag with a full one and double-checked a chart. Alex's mom resumed reading where she'd left off. Her features softened as she began reciting the familiar story.

"'It is true that Osiris was first a living king. But it is also true that the Egyptians saw little difference between the world of the living and that of the dead. . .'"

Helen shot her a quick, disapproving look, as if to say: *All this talk of death.* Alex's mom kept reading. She knew this story was her son's favourite. He always liked the ones with a hint of immortality to them. "'Osiris ruled wisely, but his brother, Set, grew jealous. Set struck down his brother and cast his body into the floodwaters of the Nile. It was faithful Isis who searched for and found the body. Using powerful magic and potent spells, she brought Osiris back to life.'"

Helen glanced over, looked away. She headed towards the door, swiping at a last speck of dust as she left. Dr Bauer shot to her feet, tossed the book aside, and glanced at the clock. *How long until the next nurse ducked her head in: Five minutes? Ten?*

Dr Bauer reached up and wrapped her left hand around the ancient scarab at her neck. She waved her right hand towards the open door and watched it snap shut. *Not enough.* She looked down at her chair. She flicked her wrist towards the door again and the chair skittered across the waxed tile and lodged itself firmly under the door handle. *Better.*

Dr Bauer took a deep breath. That was the easy part. What she was about to do was something else entirely. She wasn't sure it could be done, and she wasn't sure if it should be. She let go of the amulet and, with a trembling hand, picked up her briefcase.

She took one last look at her son, allowing herself to really see him this time. Her breath caught in her chest. He looked so small under the covers, and there were so many tubes and wires. The doctors had already begun talking to her about "moving on," about disconnecting.

"The machines are keeping him going," they told her, always careful to say "going" instead of "alive." To them, he was already gone.

But not to her.

Not yet.

A deep breath: She had to try. He was *her* son, not theirs. And she had access to more than mere machinery. She'd spent her life finding it. So many days and weeks away from him already. Days she would never get back, unless. . .

She looked over at the little table covered with cards, stuffed animals and flowers from her coworkers. She'd thank them later. She placed the vase of flowers on the floor and then swept her forearm across the table. The animals flopped on to the floor, landing with soft thuds, and the cards wafted down to join them.

Dr Bauer opened her briefcase and carefully removed a panel revealing a secret compartment. She gently lifted out the object that had been hidden inside: her life's work. The golden letters of the Lost Spells reflected the dim light of the room as she flattened the ancient cloth out on the table. Her hands were trembling more now – shaking, really.

How can I control these spells if I can't control myself?

She let out a long, slow breath, trying to expel all fear and doubt.

She glanced at the door, at the clock, and then

reached up and wrapped her left hand around her amulet again. The scarab: the symbol of rebirth, regeneration. It felt hot in her hand. On the table in front of her, the Lost Spells began to change. Soon, the golden letters were giving off more light than the room had to offer, glowing rather than reflecting. The linen lost the dull yellow tint of time and reclaimed the crisp white of long ago. Even the air seemed different, the scent of industrial cleaners brushed away by a light desert breeze.

The old magic was here. She could feel it all around her. It had travelled across the ages, and that both frightened and reassured her. Her eyes scanned the document, the ancient symbols now as clear to her as her ABCs. She found the right spell, and in a low, clear voice, she began to chant.

"Aa-Nadj Khetraak. . ."

Her voice grew louder and her grip on the amulet grew stronger. The desert breeze became a strong wind, whipping through the little room. The blinds rippled and flapped against the inside of the closed window. She reached down and held the scroll in place. She didn't realize how tightly she was clutching her amulet until thin lines of blood began to slip out from between her fingers.

Her voice was no longer alone.

She heard them now: phantom whispers, dry and raspy, emerging from the air itself and echoing her words. Her right hand no longer trembled. Instead, it brushed across the page without her even asking it to, following the lines of text.

The sheer power of it overwhelmed her. It was as if, intent on starting a campfire, she'd looked up to find the entire campsite ablaze.

At last, she reached the end. Her right hand trailed off the edge of the scroll, and with great effort, she pried her left hand from the amulet.

The wind died down. The glow of the letters faded along with the whiteness of the linen. For a few moments, the only sound was the monotonous drone of the machines. Had it worked? She raised her eyes from the scroll to look at her son.

His small body was still motionless.

She felt all the energy drain out of her. Her knees buckled and she nearly fell to the floor. That was it, then.

Out in the hallway, someone pounded on the door. Dr Bauer jumped at the sound. "This door has to stay open," a voice called from the other side. "And that TV was too loud."

"Just a second!" she called back, her voice faltering only slightly.

She looked down at the twin wounds on her bloody hand, where the copper-tipped beetle wings had punched through her skin. She grabbed a handful of tissues and quickly – with one hand and one fist – put the scroll back in its hiding place. *I've done all I can,* she thought, her head buzzing with the enormity of it.

More knocking.

"Coming!" she called, trying to find some scrap of brightness to attach to her voice. But as she started towards the door, a glimpse of movement in the corner of her eye stopped her cold.

She spun around. There it was again.

It wasn't much, just a twitch of Alex's hand. A moment later, she saw a quick nod of his chin.

She rushed across the room, tossed the chair aside, and threw open the door. "Quick," she cried. "He's awake!"

9

AWAKENING

Alex wasn't the only one waking up.

At a handful of spots around the globe, an unfortunate few would also bear witness.

Of these, a boy named Hamadi Chaltoum was merely the most tragic. His family was making him go out and get water in the middle of the night. It was an annoyance but not a surprise. Still, couldn't they at least wait till dawn? It would be there in a few hours, and then he could see where he was going.

"The moon is up," said his mother. "And you should know the way by now."

"Fine," he said. He knew it wasn't up for discussion. His baby sister was sick, and they needed to heat up more water. He would have to go to the well at the edge of the village. He took the bucket and headed out into the hot night. The moon was still bright overhead, not full but close to it. He took the main path. All around him the village slept.

His footsteps were the only sound.

This was a part of Egypt that outsiders seldom saw, in the far south near the border with Sudan. It was close to the famous tombs at Abu Simbel, true, but off the edge of the brightly coloured tourist maps. Hamadi knew well that the tourists didn't venture beyond those boundaries, beyond the little cartoon drawings of tombs and treasure. They wanted to dream of ancient rich people, not modern poor ones. When he was younger, his mother had taken him there. Not to see the sights but to beg. He was too old now, no longer cute enough. She'd take his sister soon, if she recovered.

A sound reached Hamadi's ears, and he whipped his head around. It was a dry sound, like the rustling of old wheat.

It's just the wind, he told himself.

But when he turned back, his skin told him the truth. There was no wind tonight.

Some little animal, then. Keep walking.

He quickened his pace. As he did, he passed the edge of the village. There were no more houses now, just this dirt path, worn smooth by the feet of a hundred generations. He watched it carefully. The dangers out here were the old ones: cobras, scorpions. He swung the bucket. It felt heavy and reassuring in his hand.

Friissshhhh. It was the rustling sound again, louder this time. *And closer*, thought Hamadi. He peered out into the open country to his left.

It's nothing, he told himself. *Keep moving.*

He hadn't made it two steps before he heard it again.

Frrissshh-friissshhh!

He shook his bucket and it rattled and plunked in his hand. He knew that small animals were skittish. It was quiet for a few moments, and he walked on. The well was just up ahead now.

Frrrisssshhhh-friiissshhhh-frrish!

The well was just up ahead, but so was the sound.

Whatever it was, it had passed him.

Hamadi looked into the night, and the night looked back at him. He wanted to run. Desperately. But what would he tell his mother, that there was a sound? She would laugh and send him right back out, tell him that one little baby was enough in the family.

But there *was* a sound. And it was getting closer.

"Get back!" he said, swinging his bucket in front of him. "Leave me—" But the words caught in his throat, because now he did see something. By the weak light of the falling moon, he caught a glimpse of unspeakable horror.

It was moving fast, impossibly fast.

A withered hand flashed across his vision like a cobra striking.

Now there was another sound in the night, but this was no dry rustling. This one was wet—

Desperate—

Choking—

Still.

Silence finally fell over the southern desert, and dawn rose. The village began to stir, not from the outside in or the inside out, but here and there, everybody waking at his or her own pace.

This was true of even the longest sleeps.

In the heart of the village, one family hadn't slept at all. At first, a sick baby had kept them up.

Now they waited for a boy who would never return.

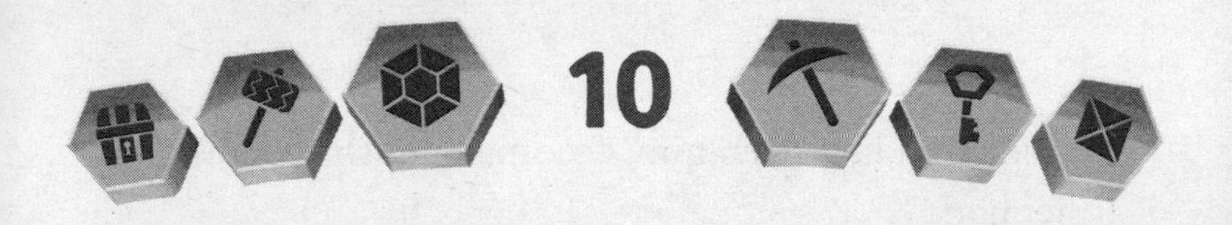

10

THE RETURNER

Alex woke up.

He woke up in the dark to the feeling of being pushed around. Another push, a quick pull, and his eyes finally blinked open.

He coughed and gasped and felt huge gulps of air enter his lungs, and opened his eyes the rest of the way.

He shut them immediately against the sudden flood of light. The single image he had at that moment, snapped like a photograph, was of his mom standing over him, face pale, with blood on her hand.

He woke up again to another tug-of-war. He couldn't say if it was an hour or a minute later, just that this time a nurse was trying to prise a paperback book from his hand.

The third time he woke up, it was to voices. He felt better this time, more alert. He slowly opened his eyes. The room was dark, with only a little dim light leaking in from the hallway. Two doctors were standing by the bed and whispering.

"This is the one I was telling you about," said one. "This kid was clinically dead. Called it myself."

"How long?"

"Two minutes was the longest, but it was the machines doing the work after that."

Alex heard the words clearly, but his mind struggled to process them.

Dead? he thought. *Like* dead *dead?*

"And now?"

"Totally normal. BP, vitals, everything."

Alex drifted off again, but he remembered the words clearly the next morning. He certainly felt normal. In fact, he felt better than he could ever remember – no pains, no pinpricks. He was waiting for his mom to arrive so he could tell her. A nurse was buzzing around the room, and the TV was on above them.

"It's a strange day, indeed!" said a newscaster with impressive hair. "Reports of unusual events are coming in from several locations. None more unusual than what happened in England, just after sunrise."

A graphic appeared at the bottom of the screen. THAT BLOODY RAIN IN LONDON, it read in large red letters.

"Several reputable sources confirm seeing, and in some cases feeling, what seemed to be blood falling from the sky in England's capital. The red drops turned back to rain before any quick-thinking Brits could get a sample of the sanguine stuff, but witnesses are standing by their gory story."

The screen flashed to an elderly man. "Oh, it was blood, all right. I was a medic in the army, so I know what it looks like, don't I? Could even smell it. Has a coppery smell. Very distinctive."

The screen flashed back to the anchor. "Now we're taking you to central Egypt, where an unidentified light source briefly turned night into day over a large swath of the Sahara desert. . ."

Alex's eyes flicked from the TV to the door.

"Alex, honey," his mom said, rushing into the room.

"Hi, Mom," he croaked.

He could feel tears in his eyes, but he wasn't even embarrassed, and he didn't push her away when she covered his mussed-up hair with kisses. The nurse retreated tactfully. And then his mom heard the TV: "We now take you to the Egyptian capital, Cairo."

Her head whipped around. Her piercing eyes quickly scanned the screen and the headlines scrolling across the bottom.

"It can't—" she began, but she abandoned the sentence. Her mouth hung slightly open as the live report continued.

"Mom, the news says—" Alex began, but she cut him off.

"Oh, don't listen to this silly stuff!"

She fumbled for the remote and clicked the TV off.

The room was silent, just the two of them again. Something had changed – Alex could still see the love in his mom's eyes, but his heart sank just a fraction as he saw the old worry lines deepen around them once more.

They ran test after test, but by Saturday morning, they could no longer justify keeping a clearly healthy boy lying in an adjustable bed wearing a paper robe. When his mom took him home, for some reason Alex couldn't get over how familiar everything seemed. The way his mom had to jiggle the key in the lock, the dinged-up mailboxes in the entryway . . . it was as if nothing had changed, as if he hadn't even been away.

As if I didn't die and come back. The words flashed through his mind, and he shook his head fiercely to clear them.

"Oh, don't do that, honey," his mom said, like always. "You know it's not good for you."

His mom was just as upset at home as she had been at the hospital. She sat down at the computer to fire off an email only to pick up her phone and rush out into the hall to make a call. She abandoned sentences halfway and riffled through the thickest and oldest books in the bookcase.

"I'm fine, Mom," said Alex. "Really."

She just smiled at him and put her hand on his

forehead absently. "You stay here and rest, OK?" she said. "I have to check on some things at work."

"But it's Saturday," Alex said, putting down the copy of *Watership Down* that Ren had given him. As weird as his mom was acting, he still didn't want her to leave.

"I won't be too long," she said. "Just need to take a look at a few things."

The tone of her voice – a little too breezy – told Alex she was holding something back. "Is there a problem with the new exhibition?" he guessed.

"You wouldn't believe me if I told you," she said, forcing a quick smile. "I'll be back as soon as I can."

"I could come with you. . ."

"NO!" she all but shouted. She paused and started again. "Not today, honey. You have a nap. Doctor's orders."

"Doctor of what?" he said.

"Egyptology," she answered. It was one of their standard jokes, and for just a moment a small, sad smile brightened her face.

"OK," he said. He wasn't tired at all, but he went into his room and climbed into bed. A minute later, he heard her talking on her phone. He caught snatches through the door: *"Ja, natürlich . . . Jetz gerade?"* It was German. He figured it was his grandmother – until the talking became shouting. *"Das ist nicht richtig! . . . War er verletzt? . . . Nein, Doktor!"*

Doktor? thought Alex.

The call ended.

The door slammed.

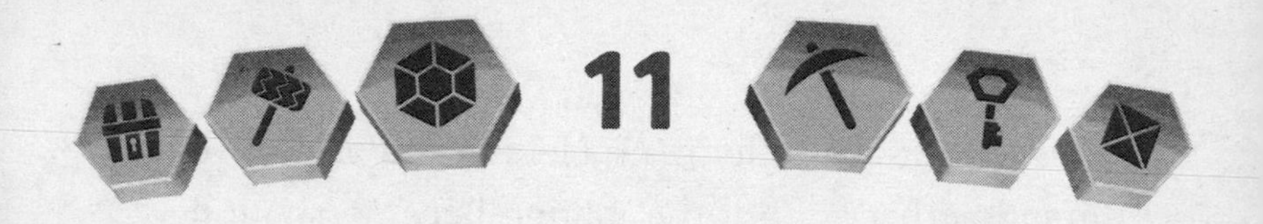

11

THE HYENA

Back in the museum, a new guard named Jonas held up a large leather bag. "It's OK," he said. "Just bringing something to one of the guys."

Oscar had been leaning against the wall next to the thick steel door of the security room. He pushed himself free and took a few steps forward. He looked closely at his fellow guard. They were wearing the same uniform but were separated by decades of experience. "Listen, I know you're new here," he said. "What's it been, a couple weeks? But this room is for authorized personnel only – and you ain't it."

Jonas didn't budge. Oscar cocked his head slightly, assessing the situation. He wasn't used to having his orders ignored by newbies. The two guards sized each other up: both big men, one younger, the other more experienced.

"Is there a problem?" said Oscar.

"No problem," said Jonas. "It's just, I think he'll want this."

He unzipped the bag and reached in with one hand. Then he let the bag fall to the floor.

"What *is* that?" said Oscar, his disgust evident in both his tone and his expression. "A dog's head or something?"

Jonas smiled. He raised the leathery brown object up and began slipping the mask on.

Oscar almost retched. It *was* a dog's head – or something like one, anyway. But the fur was long gone, and the skin seemed as close to beef jerky as leather.

"This isn't Halloween," he said, shaking off the initial shock. Oscar was a trained fighter and an ex-Marine. He even bore a certain resemblance to a middle-aged Muhammad Ali. To say he wasn't easily scared was an understatement. And today, he was guarding the security room. Inside were the controls and monitors for all the cameras in the museum, along with the mainframe controlling the alarms and time locks.

It was an important job. He stood his ground.

"Not Halloween," said Jonas, his face covered now and his voice distorted by the dry, hollow mask. "No holiday at all."

Oscar vaguely recognized the face as a hyena's from some long-ago nature show. The skin was very old, dried and stretched. The expression was a grotesque leering smile. Oscar's eyes darted towards the alarm button on the wall.

He lunged for it.

The man in the mask raised his hand and Oscar felt his fingers crunch, jammed backwards as if he'd thrust them into a concrete wall instead of empty air. Gasping from the pain, he tried to pull his hand back but couldn't. He tried to turn, tried to shout, tried to do anything, but he couldn't. He was frozen, pressed in place as if by the air itself. Out of the corner of his eye, he saw the man in the mask slowly closing his outstretched hand. And as the fingers closed, Oscar felt the breath being squeezed from his lungs.

*

Elsewhere in the museum – barely a strangled cry away – Alex's mom had just shut down the new exhibition. The curtains were back up. The signs on the front, still warm from the printer, read: CLOSED FOR REPAIRS: WILL REOPEN SOON! She wasn't sure either of those statements was true.

"OK, walk me through it again, Cris," she said, turning to Ren's dad. "Everything so far."

They were standing in a small room, just off to the side of the one housing the Lost Spells.

Mr Duran took a deep breath. "Well, the Book of the Dead basically looks like it was made last Tuesday. The cloth is way too supple and most of the discolouration is gone. Three of the four canopic jars have fallen over. That beetle encased in amber, in the jewellery display? Hector swears he saw its legs moving. And this. . ." He trailed off.

They both looked down at the plain little time-battered coffin in front of them. It was open, displaying a small mummy that until recently had lain straight as a board. The mummy was now slightly curled, and on its side, like a sleeping child who had shifted in the night.

Dr Bauer clenched her hands and felt a jab

of pain in the left, which was wrapped tightly in medical tape.

They walked slowly back to the main room.

"This is crazy stuff, Maggie. We need to understand what's going on before we can fix it."

"*If* we can fix it," she said. "It's not just here. I've had calls from Cairo, London, the poor guy filling in for Todtman in Berlin. . ."

"It's on the news, too," he said. "It's all they're talking about in the office. All the major collections are having problems."

"Probably some of the smaller ones, too," she said. "Just easier for them to keep it quiet."

He looked at her seriously, but she looked away. She was barely holding it together, and she couldn't risk him seeing the guilt and panic she was feeling.

I had to save Alex's life was the thought that kept running through her head. She'd known there'd be a price to pay.

"You know what I was thinking, though?" Cris said. "We all use the same methods, all handle our artefacts the same way. We even use a lot of the same products. What if. . ."

He's still looking for a scientific explanation, she thought. *But he must at least suspect.*

"Cris?" she said, and in that moment when she looked up and met his eyes, she considered telling him everything. She wanted to. She trusted him. But he was a mechanical engineer: 75 per cent scientist, 25 per cent master craftsman, and 100 per cent the last person in the world who would believe in magic.

"Listen, Maggie, I don't want to sound harsh. I know you got a lot going on. I think it's amazing, the news about Alex. We're all so happy about that. But you need to focus, all right? You've been freaked out all day, and it's starting to freak me out, too."

"I know; I'm sorry," she said. But she knew that she wasn't the thing freaking him out.

What was freaking him out was not having all the answers, for once.

What was freaking *her* out was having some of them.

They heard footsteps approaching in the closed, quiet exhibition and looked over as the museum's newest guard entered the room.

"Mr Duran?" said Jonas.

"Yeah, that's me," he said.

"They need you over in Greek sculpture. Sounds serious."

Cris gave Maggie a look: *What now?* "Be right back," he said.

Once he was gone, she looked over at the Book of the Dead. That's when she realized the guard was still standing there. "Can I help you?" she asked.

He reached behind him and began to close the glass door.

"Leave that open, please," she said. "We're having ventilation issues."

"No, we're not," said Jonas as the door swung shut.

He was holding something behind his back, and now he swung it around. It was a battered leather case, about the size of a bowling bag. It was against museum policy for guards to carry personal items around on duty, but the smirk on his face told her that he knew that already.

"What is that?" she asked as he unzipped the bag and reached inside.

"Allow me to show you," he replied, pulling the ghastly lump of sagging skin free.

Of course, she thought as he slipped the hyena mask over his head.

Hyenas were scavengers – it made sense that he'd wait for her to track down the Lost Spells, then come out to tear them away from her. She'd only heard of this man before – seen the one blurry crime scene photo that existed – but she knew all about his underground organization. She knew who she was looking at, and it wasn't a man named Jonas.

There was no Jonas.

"Al-Dab'u," she said.

"Dr Bauer," he said, giving the mask one final adjustment.

She shot a look at the ceiling. The metal disc above the Lost Spells should have been ringed with the red lights of the lasers, but the lenses were dark. Had she forgotten to switch them back on after her "repairs"? She looked at the cameras, turned in now and facing the walls. Slowly, she reached up for her amulet with her bandaged hand. She shifted her grip slightly so that the wings wouldn't find the wounds they'd made.

"I'm glad we understand each other," said Al-Dab'u.

His right hand shot out, flexing a power much greater than mere muscle. Dr Bauer's feet left the ground and her slender frame flew backwards and slammed against the wall. Display cases on either side of her rattled as the wind left her lungs.

Al-Dab'u advanced towards her, but he hesitated as he saw her hand tighten around the scarab.

An information plaque flew off the wall and informed Al-Dab'u's head that it weighed 6.2 pounds and was made of steel.

He staggered sideways, reaching up to straighten out his mask. He balled his hand into a fist, and the very air seemed to clamp down on Maggie's throat.

Two thoughts filled her mind. *The Lost Spells.* She could not allow this man to take them. *And Alex.* She needed to get back to him.

She'd been gone too long already.

12

TAKEN

When Alex went to bed that night, his mother wasn't home.

When he got up for a glass of water two hours later, she still hadn't returned.

He checked the living-room table for a note. No note, but he found a gold-paint pen and a few scraps of what looked like old cloth. As he bundled up the scraps to toss out, he saw the faded cover of a book underneath, *Legend of the Death Walkers.*

He wasn't that tired – he'd hardly been tired at

all since he'd returned from the hospital – and he was determined to wait up for his mom. He flipped open the book. He was expecting a novel and was surprised to discover that it was a very old history book. He flipped to chapter one: "Who Were the Death Walkers?"

According to legend, the Death Walkers were a group of evil men with strong spirits. They knew they would fail the weighing of the heart, so after death, they used their powerful wills to cling to the edge of the afterlife. There they remain, the tales say, struggling to hang on and desperately waiting for an opportunity to escape.

Evil men with powerful wills . . . it reminded Alex of something, and he flipped to the table of contents. And there it was, chapter four: "The Stung Man."

Cool, he thought, and settled down on the couch to read as he waited for his mom.

He woke up to the sound of someone knocking on the door: *DONK! DONK! DONK!*

Alex looked around the apartment in the dim morning light.

"Mom," he called. "Door!"

No response. He looked around again. Nothing had been moved. The keys weren't on the peg by the door.

DONK! DONK! DONK!

"Anyone home?" a man called from the other side. The sound mixed with the neighbour's corgi barking its head off.

Alex stumbled towards the door.

"Uh, who is it?" he shouted.

"Police!" came the voice.

Police? he thought. *What's going on?*

Half asleep still, he wasn't afraid, only confused.

Alex looked through the peephole and saw another eye looking in. The eye pulled back and a man's head came into view. He had Middle Eastern features that Alex thought might be Egyptian. He wasn't wearing a uniform, but then he flashed a badge in front of the peephole.

"MOM!" Alex called again.

No answer.

The confusion was turning to fear.

No, Alex thought. *Oh please no.*

"Open the door, please," called the man. He sounded either tired or annoyed, possibly both.

Alex undid the first lock: *click!* "Do you know where my mom is?"

"That's what we need to talk about."

His name was Detective Hussein, and as soon as he told Alex he regretted to inform him that his mother had disappeared from the museum, the investigation began. As he did a thorough sweep of the small apartment, he peppered Alex with questions.

"So she just got up and left for work, and that was the last you saw of her?" the detective asked.

"Yeah," said Alex. "Pretty much."

"And you're sure she didn't call? Email? Text? Anything?"

Alex shook his head. But just to be sure he checked his email. And his phone. And his voice mail. And his email again.

Nothing. Not a word.

He felt helpless and collapsed on to the couch.

"Where is she?" Alex asked. His voice broke on the last word, but he didn't care.

"We don't know," said Hussein. "Something happened yesterday. We have your mom on video entering the museum."

Alex fired off the questions as fast as he thought

of them: "What do you mean 'something happened'? *What* happened? You saw her entering the museum, so when did she leave?"

Hussein put his hand up in a stop sign, and for some reason that made Alex angry. *Are you a traffic cop or a detective?* he wanted to yell. *Tell me where she is!*

"We don't know. Cris Duran says he saw her in the Egypt wing yesterday afternoon. But it's not on the cameras. We don't have her leaving, either. We've been going over it for hours."

"Yesterday afternoon?" said Alex. He'd been waiting all that time. He could have been looking for her. *They* could have been looking for her! "Why'd you wait so long?"

"It was Saturday. People just thought she went home to be with you. But that was before we knew something else was missing."

Alex got a bad feeling.

"What?" he managed to say.

"A scroll. Very old. Some kind of spells."

"The Lost Spells," said Alex. His anger had turned to dread now, like hot water suddenly running cold.

"Yeah, those."

"She didn't take them," said Alex. "She wouldn't."

"We don't think she did. She had plenty of opportunities before that."

"Wait, you mean. . . ?"

"I'm sorry, Alex."

The cold water turned to ice.

If he hadn't been sitting down, he would have fallen.

"Did you hear me?" said Hussein.

Alex looked at him closely. For a second, he didn't even remember who this man was. "Hear what?"

"What I just said." The detective repeated himself, very slowly: "We think she's been taken."

Alex rode to the museum like a tranquillized animal.

He remembered getting in the detective's car and getting out of it, but nothing in between except the smell of old coffee. He was operating in the same sort of steady low-grade panic that people report after tornadoes or earthquakes. He started to come out of it as they headed up the broad front steps. "What are you going to do?" he asked Hussein.

"We're going to find your mom."

Alex looked up at the detective and nodded. "OK," he said. "Good." They reached the front doors, manned not by museum employees but by a pair of beefy uniformed NYPD officers.

"Detective," said the closest one, nodding to Hussein.

"Officer," said Hussein, nodding back.

They took a sharp right towards the Egyptian wing. Alex saw bright yellow police tape in front of the entrance. It took him another five or six steps to spot the man standing behind it, because he was wearing all black.

"Detective," Alex said, stopping in his tracks, a memory rushing back to him.

"Yeah?" said Hussein, stopping half a step further on.

"My mom got a phone call before she left yesterday."

Alex couldn't believe he hadn't mentioned that yet. He gave his head a vicious shake – like a dog with a chew toy. He needed to get it together, for his mom.

"She was speaking German," he said with a look towards Todtman. "And she was really upset."

"Right," said Hussein. "Interesting. You can tell me about it later."

Later? And just like that, it hit Alex. The

detective didn't consider him a partner in this case. He considered him baggage. Babysitting. Alex's head dropped, his shoulders slumped.

Hussein lifted up the yellow tape so Alex could get through. As he ducked under, Todtman walked towards him, lowering his phone from his ear.

"I'm sorry, Alex," Todtman said, addressing him as if he were a longtime friend instead of a near stranger. "I should have been here."

Alex stared at him, his suspicion growing. Of course he was claiming he wasn't here.

"Anything new, Detective?" said Todtman.

Don't tell him anything! thought Alex.

"Nothing yet," said Hussein.

"Well, let me know if I can help in any way," said Todtman.

"I will, Doctor. And do me a favour?"

"Yes, Detective?"

"Don't go anywhere."

"I don't intend to," said Todtman. He looked down at Alex and bent his face into something like a sympathetic smile. Then he put his phone back to his ear and turned away. As he did, something swung into sight under the open collar of his shirt. It wasn't much, just a flash of old copper and a hint of blue stone, but Alex recognized it immediately.

His mom's scarab.

He was sure of it.

Hussein headed into the Egyptian wing, and Alex had no choice but to follow. He shot one more look at Todtman, still whispering mysteriously into his phone.

They reached the room where the Lost Spells had been. It reminded Alex of Grand Central Terminal. Forensics investigators were walking back and forth across the room in purposeful, criss-crossing paths. Their legs made *shush-shush* sounds in their baggy plastic suits. They were collecting evidence – and there seemed to be plenty of it.

"What have you got?" said Hussein to the nearest plastic suit.

The woman inside shook her head. "What haven't we got?"

"That's not an answer, Barb," he said.

"OK," she said. "First off, some psycho moved a mummy. Moved. A. Mummy. Then there's the information plaque on the floor. No prints, but we sent the swabs on ahead."

"DNA?"

"Yeah, as near as we can tell, dog DNA."

Hussein shook his head and frowned. "We're gonna have to rerun that."

"Sure," said Barb. "We can do that right after we source the scorpions."

"Scorpions?" said Hussein, quickly scanning the floor.

"Yeah, two of them, in the next room."

"Exhibits, you mean."

"Living," she said, "and aggressive. I've got 'em in specimen jars if you want to see 'em."

"This is crazy," said Hussein. "OK, what about the case? How'd they get the scroll?"

Alex looked over at it. His brain was reeling again. *Dog DNA?* He stared at the case, trying to focus on something.

"That's the weirdest part," said Barb.

Hussein raised his eyebrows. "I find that hard to believe."

"The case is completely intact – still locked, still sealed. And utterly empty."

13

THE MISSION

"We contacted your aunt and uncle, and they'll be here by the end of the day," said Hussein. He didn't want to ditch the kid, but he had work to do. And the kid had a lot more questions for him than he had answers. "I can get an officer to stay with you if. . ."

"Don't worry about it," said Alex. "I know my way around here."

"Don't go far," said the detective. That seemed responsible enough.

After a few wrong turns, Hussein found his way

to the small office where he'd been set up. He found the key and opened the door. The room was dark, and he flipped the light switch by the door: nothing. *Bulb must be out*, he thought. He walked carefully towards the desk, the outline of a small lamp just visible in the shadows.

The door suddenly slammed shut behind him. Hussein swung around but saw nothing. The room was totally dark now except for a few lines of light slipping in through the slats of the blinds.

"Very funny," he said. "Jackson, is that you?"

The lamp clicked on. It wasn't Jackson. The light was weak, but the face of the man sitting at the desk was very pale and Hussein could see every fleshy fold.

"Wait, am I in the wrong office?" said Hussein.

The man's left hand slowly wrapped around one of two shiny objects hanging from his neck. "You are in the perfect place, Detective," he said in his crisp German accent.

The police investigation had, for all practical purposes, just come to a close.

It hadn't taken Alex long to get tired of waiting around the office. He slipped into spy mode –

determined to see what the investigation was uncovering. By the end of the day, no one seemed to know anything more, but he did find Ren. She was leaving Medieval Art just as he was heading in. The near collision resulted in a near hug – which Alex honestly wouldn't have minded so much. The sight of his best friend filled him with a wave of relief and gratitude. It wasn't that long ago that it seemed like he'd never see her again. . . But there was no time for that stuff now.

He dragged her to a bench outside the museum, on the edge of Central Park. It was a beautiful evening, and he felt better than ever – no aches, no pains. All this would have been great except that there was a giant hole in the centre of his world.

"I heard everyone at the museum talking. What did the detective say?" asked Ren.

"They think whoever took the Spells took my mom," he said. "Maybe she was just in the way, and they'll try to ransom her back to the museum. Or they might need her to help them 'find a buyer' for the Lost Spells."

He felt himself getting angrier as he talked. "I knew something weird was going on with that exhibit – that stupid exhibit!"

Ren flinched at the volume.

"Sorry."

Ren looked around, as if she were checking out the park. Alex knew she was trying to find the right thing to say. "The police will find her," she said at last.

Now it was Alex's turn to be quiet. He thought about it. He needed to be honest with himself about this. "They won't," he said.

"Don't say that."

"They're not even trying, Ren!" The words bubbled up from some deep well of frustration within him. "There are a ton of them here, but all they're doing is sitting around. Talking."

"About the case?"

"About the Yankees!"

Ren shook her head, but she didn't try to argue this time. "They weren't doing much when I was up there, either."

Alex looked at her. She sounded sad about it. He wanted her to sound angry – as angry and frustrated as him. "I think Todtman has my mom's necklace."

"Really?" said Ren, her voice rising with surprise. "Did you see it?"

"Part of it," he admitted. "But the detective

wouldn't even listen when I tried to tell him about it."

Ren shook her head: "Well, that *is* stupid."

For the first time, Alex thought he heard some anger in her voice.

He tried to fan the flame a little. "Yeah, *so* stupid."

"And you know that Todtman's in charge of the exhibition now, right?"

"WHAT?" said Alex. He couldn't believe it. "And they're just sitting around, waiting for a call. A call that might never come. Until then, where's my mom? Who's she with? What kind of people would do all this?"

"Bad people," said Ren. "Or crazy."

A shudder shot through Alex. A plan was taking shape in his head, and he needed Ren.

Ren looked at him. Her expression was still uncertain. And then her eyes got wide with recognition. "*Oh,*" she said.

"Yes," said Alex.

"*We* need to do something."

"Yes!" he practically shouted.

"We do know the museum a lot better than they do."

"And I know my mom so much better, and at least we know what the Lost Spells are, which they don't even seem to."

"And if they missed Todtman, what else did they miss?" Ren's voice was getting almost as loud as Alex's now. "I have an idea," she said. "I heard something. . ."

Alex smiled.

She was the hardest-working, most focused girl on the Upper East Side.

He was the leading expert on ancient Egypt, age twelve and under.

And they had a mission.

14

SNEAKING OUT

In the forty-eight hours since his mother went missing, Alex had discovered only one thing: Even the most important mission can be sidelined by a well-meaning aunt.

Alex was stuck in his new "room", which was actually his uncle's office. He was playing *Dragon Stryke II: Out of the Sun* on a semi-ancient computer and waiting until it was late enough for him to sneak out. His dragon crested a mountain peak. Alex flapped its wings one more time and then took a quick look out the window at the old, rusty fire escape. *Will that thing even hold me?* When he looked back, his dragon was engulfed in flames.

He scanned the screen to see where the attack had come from. It had come from out of the sun, of course. A fire-breathing red dragon had swooped down from above. Alex watched the crumpled, smoking frame of his lightning-breathing blue dragon crash into the mountaintop. In the end-of-game quiet, he listened carefully. Aunt Adele was still in the hall complaining loudly about one of her co-workers.

Alex looked around the room and saw the confines of his new world. The thin foam mattress he slept on was rolled up in the corner. His clothes were stuffed into an old cardboard box marked *Taxes*, and *Legend of the Death Walkers* was propped up by the window along with a few of his mom's other things.

He turned back to the computer and hit reset on the game. His blue dragon re-formed in mid-air and breathed out its trademark lightning bolt. The dragon was brand new, all the damage from the last game gone. A fresh start: full health. *Just like me,* he thought, scanning the sky for enemies.

The TV blared to life out in the living room and was briefly muted. "Alex! TV!" screamed Adele.

"No thanks!" he shouted back. "Playing *Dragon Stryke*! Probably going to turn in early! Tired!"

The volume roared back to its normal, neighbour-shaking level. Alex locked the door and checked the time: a little past seven thirty. He was running late. He saved the game, turned off the light, and grabbed his backpack.

Alex pushed the chair in and stepped over to the window. He tried to be quiet. The old window groaned but slid up with surprising ease. But as soon as the window opened, the door did, too. Alex looked back. It was his cousin Luke. His room was on the other side of the thin office wall. *Busted*, thought Alex. His cousin had been surprisingly cool to him so far, but Alex figured that was over now.

"Where you going?" said Luke. Dressed in his standard array of workout gear, he looked like an ad for Under Armour.

"Uh, nowhere?" Alex ventured.

"Yeah, right," said Luke. "Don't sweat it. Why do you think that window slides open so easy? I use it, too."

"So you're not going to. . ." Alex couldn't bring

himself to say "tell". It sounded too babyish around his cool, cocky older cousin.

"Nah," said Luke. "Just wanted to let you know there's a missing step halfway down. Kind of dangerous in the dark, so watch out."

And just like that, he was gone.

Alex slid one leg through and stepped gingerly on to the battered metal fire escape. The whole structure swayed slightly and Alex glanced back into the safety of the office.

What the heck, he thought. *You only live twice.*

He slid the window closed behind him and crept carefully over to the steep metal stairs. The fire escape swayed a little more, but he climbed down to the second-floor platform without the whole thing peeling off the building. The missing step was tricky, but he got past it without breaking anything thanks to Luke's warning. An extendable ladder led down to the alleyway. It let out a single, strangled-cat screech as Alex pushed it down. A light came on in the window next to him and he scampered down quickly without risking a look.

The ladder ended a good four feet above the alleyway. Alex lowered himself and dropped. He landed safely next to the recycling bins, then straightened up, wiped his hands on his jeans, and headed out into the darkening city.

Alex turned the corner and jogged to the bus stop. There was an emergency staff meeting at the Met, after hours at 8:00 p.m. "Crisis control," Ren had called it. Everyone involved in the new exhibition would be there, packed into the main conference room. Everyone. That was their window of opportunity – apart from his actual window – and he couldn't be late.

The M96 bus pulled up two minutes later. He got a seat and tried to think about absolutely anything other than his mom. *"You have powerful magic, my son. You have summoned the Ancient Ones. . ."* He shook his head so sharply that the man sitting next to him shifted subtly away.

He took that day's *New York Post* out of his backpack to reread the story. "Trouble at the Met: Cursed Exhibit or Pyramid Scheme?" Their piece on the heist and his mom's disappearance had been serious, but this one was written mostly for laughs. He already knew the parts about the "sleepless mummy" and "tipsy jars", so he skipped down and reread the end: *The Met isn't the only famous museum having mummy issues.*

The Museum of Egyptian Antiquities in Cairo was recently shut down due to what officials there dubbed "mass psychosis".

He stuffed the paper back in his pack. It reminded him of the news reports from the morning he'd woken up: blood rain, night turning to day. Now the Lost Spells had been stolen, his mom was missing, and an entire museum was closed.

But that was wrong. He knew it was wrong. His mom's disappearance wasn't an item on a list. It *was* the list. It was the paper it was written on and the pen it was written with. His mom's absence was everything. And Alex would do anything to find her.

"What took you so long?" asked Ren.

It was 8:03. She was holding the door to the staff entrance open.

"I literally could not have got here any faster!" Alex protested. "I ran all the way from the bus stop."

"You ran? From the crosstown stop?"

"Yeah."

Ren frowned. "You need to be careful. You have your medicine, right?"

He ignored the question. It wasn't his own health he was worried about now. The thought that his mom might be suffering had entered his mind, and now it refused to leave. She might be tied up in the dark or hurt or—

"We need to be quiet," Ren cautioned as they headed into the shadowy hush of the closed museum. "It echoes less if we walk along the walls."

But they barely made it a hundred yards before they were spotted.

"Where are you two going?" said Oscar. Alex had always liked Oscar. The guard had been working at the museum for ages, had seen them grow up – and basically let them do whatever they wanted.

"Dad has a meeting," said Ren.

"Yeah, I heard about that. I'm sure they'll get all this straightened out."

"How'd you get that?" said Ren, staring at the clean white cast on Oscar's hand.

The guard looked embarrassed. "Honestly? No idea," he said. "Think I must have fallen and hit my head and my hand at the same time. That's my best guess, anyway. I did have a headache."

"Can we sign it?"

Oscar shook his head. "Not professional," he said. "How you doing, Alex?"

Alex gave him a weak thumbs-up.

“He doesn’t like to talk about it,” said Ren, tugging him along.

“Course,” said Oscar. “You two take care. And don’t set off any alarms on the way to the office.”

“We won’t!” promised Ren as they headed towards the elevator.

As soon as Oscar turned the corner, they changed course and hurried on towards the Egyptian wing.

“I guess it’s only the guards assigned to the new exhibition who are in the meeting,” whispered Alex.

“Yeah,” said Ren, looking around like they were in lion country. “We’ll have to be more careful.”

They avoided a second guard near the main entrance and made it to Egypt by 8:10.

The wing was dim and quiet. Alex felt a chill ripple through him as they edged deeper into the half-light. This was no longer friendly terrain, no longer his mom’s extended office. This was a crime scene now. A place where he’d seen things. At least he thought he had. Those last moments before his collapse seemed like a dream to him now.

“Watch out for scorpions,” said Ren.

Alex knew it was supposed to be a joke, something to break the tension, but neither of them laughed. The eerie quiet wrapped around them. Alex could hear Ren's hushed breathing between the soft slap of their footsteps. It was a silence that reminded him they were on their own: no help, no witnesses.

"OK, so the police have been all over this place," he said. Even at half his normal volume, his voice seemed to fill the room. "And then the cleaning crews." He side-eyed the little tomb where he'd collapsed, and picked up his pace.

"Slow down," said Ren. "You always . . . you, like, practically run by that thing."

"I just don't like it," he said. He remembered the feeling of lying on the cold floor, the helplessness. The jackal's eyes. But he didn't let his thoughts get sidetracked this time. "So we're not going to find anything, like, lying on the floor. But we might see something out of place or. . ."

"I know," said Ren. "I have some theories."

Alex watched her pull a notebook from her messenger bag.

"What did you do, make a list?"

"Two pages," she said. Alex looked over and saw the neatly printed items filling the first page. Back in school, Ren was always making lists. She didn't show them to anyone else, because she knew they'd make fun of her. Plus Ten Ren. But she showed them to Alex, because she knew he wouldn't. All it proved to him was that he had the right partner.

"First I want to show you the little mummy," she said. "Because it's freaky."

The curtain was up over the doorway, but there was no guard in front of it. There honestly wasn't much left to guard. Alex wasn't sure he wanted to step through, but Ren's busy efficiency made him feel safer somehow.

"Speaking of freaky," he said as they walked past the Stung Man's sarcophagus.

They passed the empty case in the next room and headed straight into the side room that held the mummy child. Alex had seen it just a few days earlier, and he noticed the change immediately. Alex stared at it through the glass. "You know what it looks like?" he whispered.

"What?"

"Like it can't sleep. Like it's trying to get comfortable."

"She," said Ren. "Like *she* can't sleep. The sign says she was a little girl who died from disease."

"You're not making this any less spooky," said Alex.

"Spooky," said Ren, holding up her notebook, "is not on the list."

"OK then, what is?"

"OK, first clue: cameras. They're everywhere" – she waved the notebook in the general direction of the ceiling – "but the detective told you there was nothing on them."

"So?"

"So, step one: blind spots. We need to figure out where they are, and what might have happened in them."

Both kids looked up at the security cameras around the room.

"Wait," said Alex. "Do you hear that?"

Ren cocked her head, lifting one ear slightly to listen. "Sounds like cereal in a box."

"Or dirt in a shovel," offered Alex.

"But where's it—"

They both turned and looked back down at the little mummy.

She was looking right at them.

Her whole body had shifted, and her empty eye sockets gazed blankly up at them.

"Holy—" began Alex.

"What the—" began Ren, her voice rising.

And that's when the entire museum went dark.

*

Someone screamed. Alex thought it was Ren, but he could not rule out the possibility that it was him.

Or the mummy.

"The power went out!" shouted Ren, her voice stretched with panic.

Alex heard her footsteps as she slowly backed away from the coffin in the darkness. He did the same, his hand stretched out behind him, feeling for the wall.

"What do we do?" said Ren.

Alex looked around but saw only blackness. He knew this wing well, but well enough to find his way out in the dark?

As if in answer, an emergency light clicked on along the far wall, casting a weak glow that left much of the room in shadow. Alex could hear the faint sound of far-off shouting as employees and guards scrambled to follow the museum's blackout protocols: securing the exits and the most valuable paintings.

"Ren, let's get out of here!" he called.

She was already moving.

They sprinted through the room where the Lost Spells had been, but they came to a halt in the one housing the Stung Man. A harsh grinding sound filled the room. In the weak glow of another emergency light, they couldn't see where the noise was coming from.

"What is that?" said Ren, nervously scanning the room.

Alex saw it now. He opened his mouth, but nothing came out. He did manage to point. Ren followed his finger – straight towards the Stung Man's sarcophagus.

She took a quick, sharp breath, but her voice failed her, too.

They both watched in silent horror as the heavy stone lid of the Stung Man's sarcophagus slowly slid back.

15

THE STUNG MAN

The canopic jars lined up in front of the sarcophagus began to shake.

Alex watched the black gap grow as the lid continued to grind backwards. He thought he could see something stirring inside.

With his body suspended between paralysis and flight, Alex's mind was working overtime. It was clear to him now. His suspicion had become a certainty. This wasn't about camera angles or death's door hallucinations. He'd been avoiding the word this whole time, but he needed to accept it. "It's magic, Ren. It is."

Ren shook her head slowly, her eyes fixed on the exit. They'd have to go right by the sarcophagus if they wanted to get out of here.

As they watched, the ancient jars rattled like maracas and the five-hundred-pound lid yawned open to the ragged soundtrack of rock grinding on rock.

And then Alex saw the hand.

The heavy stone lid of the sarcophagus fell to the floor with a loud *Kronk!* In the weak light, Alex saw two smaller lids inside, both pushed up and away. *How much strength did that take?* The hand rose up from the deep shadows within. Ragged wrappings frayed and fell aside as the fingers curled for the first time in millennia. Alex watched in frozen horror as the entire arm emerged, hooking itself over the edge of the carved stone and pulling the rest of the body into the light. The canopic jars on the floor below were shaking so violently that they seemed like they might explode.

It was the Stung Man. His skin was visible in the places where his wrappings had given way, but it looked nothing like the skin of the other mummies

Alex had seen. It wasn't stretched and dried and stained by time. It was livid and covered with swollen welts. The Stung Man turned and stared into the room, not with empty sockets but with wet, sinister eyes.

"Run!" screamed Ren. "We have to run!"

The path out of the room would take them within just a few feet of the creature, but they couldn't go back. The other mummy was back there – and who knew what else.

Alex took one more horrified look: The Stung Man was staggering to his feet. Soon, he'd be free.

Ren took off, and Alex followed a split second later, his feet reacting faster than his brain.

The Stung Man took a slow, clumsy swipe at them as they passed, and Alex ducked to avoid the blow.

Almost to the door now.

It slammed shut just before they reached it. Ren was running so fast she couldn't stop in time, and she bounced against the thick safety glass. Alex skidded to a halt and grabbed Ren's shoulders to steady her.

"No!" she gasped. He could hear the fear in her voice.

She began to tug wildly at the handle in front of her.

Alex wrapped his hands alongside hers on the handle and pulled with all his strength, but it wasn't giving.

"Stay awhile," a man's voice called behind them. "You're just in time."

A figure in a guard's uniform stepped from the shadows in the far corner of the room, and for a second, Alex felt a wash of relief. But then panic surged again. The guard's body was that of a man. But the head . . . the head. . .

Alex felt his knees begin to give. The man had the desiccated head of a hyena. Ren whimpered beside him, and fear took over Alex's body. Spots swam in his vision and his head began to loll back, as if his neck had turned to rubber.

Then he felt a sudden impact.

Ren had collapsed backwards into him.

You can't pass out, he thought. *I was going to do that!*

He hooked his arms under Ren's, elbows to armpits, and tried to drag her upright.

"Yes, stay right there," the man in the mask said.

Alex had no intention of doing so. His head

whipped from the guard across the room to the mummy struggling up from his stone bed.

"Stay still," the guard repeated.

Alex understood now. This man was no guard. He tried to lift Ren to her feet but he wasn't strong enough and she just hung there, dead weight. He shook her. Her eyes snapped open and she looked up at him.

"You gotta get up, Ren!"

But just as she began to gather her feet underneath her, the man in the mask extended his right hand, palm down, and pressed it towards the floor.

A great force hit Alex and Ren and flattened them against the ground. Alex tried to stand, tried to push Ren up, but it felt as if someone had dropped a mattress on them.

The Stung Man, however, rose to his full height. Alex could see his face through the filthy wrappings. The skin was neither living nor dead but some grotesque approximation of both, and the entire left side was lumpy and swollen.

Scorpion stings, Alex realized in horror.

"Let us go!" shouted Alex, even though he didn't understand how he was being held. He tried to roll towards the wall. Nothing.

"Let *her* go!" he yelled.

The hyena head tilted back in laughter. "The two of you are barely a snack as it is. He needs to *feed*."

Alex flicked his eyes towards Ren. Her face was tight with terror. They were laid out before the sarcophagus like two pigs in a blanket on a tray.

"He may not consume your bodies," said the guard. "But he will certainly take your souls."

The disfigured corpse stepped clear of its long confinement and took an unsteady step in their direction. He reached out and pulled a handful of empty air back to him. Even through the struggle and panic, Alex felt a glimmer of recognition. He remembered his own waking moments in the hospital: groggy and disoriented, unsure what his body had in store for him.

Alex tried to stand, roll, kick. Nothing.

And then. . .

BRRAACCKK!

The door behind them flew open so hard the safety glass cracked.

With a sudden jerk, the invisible weight holding him down lifted.

Alex leapt to his feet.

He reached down for Ren, but she was already scrambling up.

They half stumbled and half ran towards the open door. Alex was hoping to see the police, or at least a real guard. Instead he got. . .

"Todtman!" called the man in the mask.

"Al-Dab'u," called the German.

The Stung Man came to an unsteady halt and looked from one to the other.

They're working together! thought Alex, his brain sloshing with adrenaline.

"Oh no!" moaned Ren.

"Stay out of this!" called the guard. "This is no place for frail scholars. Let me do my work."

"You know I can't," said Todtman.

Wait, thought Alex. *They know each other. . .*

"Then you will suffer the same fate!"

. . . but they aren't working together. . .

"*Nicht heute,*" breathed Todtman.

Alex rummaged the cupboards of his overheated brain, found the few German words his grandmother had taught him: *Nicht heute.* Not today.

Todtman reached up towards the open collar of his button-down shirt. The emergency light reflected off something in his hand. He held an amulet – it wasn't the scarab but some sort of bird – and thrust it towards Al-Dab'u.

Al-Dab'u's body lifted and jerked as a great unseen force seemed to hit him. "You . . . I . . . didn't," stammered Al-Dab'u, and his hands flew to his temples. "Get . . . out . . . of . . . my . . . head," he managed, struggling to complete each word.

The Stung Man lost interest in the two combatants and turned back towards his young meal.

"Let's go!" yelled Ren, yanking on Alex's sleeve.

As they raced towards Todtman, the froggy man's eyes widened in horror. "Get down!" he screamed, diving to his right.

Alex and Ren threw themselves on the ground just as a massive display case hurtled over them and landed in a crash of glass and metal right where Todtman had been standing.

Alex and Ren leapt to their feet once more, Alex's heart pounding now, and his breathing heavy. The twisted metal bulk of the display case filled the doorway – they'd never get over it in time. Their only chance now was the far door, but they'd have to get past the Stung Man and Al-Dab'u to reach it.

Alex and Ren locked eyes for one fleeting second,

and Alex could see his fear and disbelief reflected back at him in her face. "We have to," he managed. She locked her jaw and nodded. The Stung Man jerked in confusion as the two kids barrelled towards him. He staggered for a step then found his feet, crouched low, and brought his long arms up in a vicious lunge.

"Watch out, Ren!"

Alex dived for the floor just under the Stung Man's reach, his momentum propelling him in a belly slide across the polished marble. He slammed into the wall near the far door in a tangle of arms and legs. Ren reached him a second later, still on her feet. She grabbed his hand and yanked him out of the way just as a stone chunk from the broken sarcophagus exploded against the wall where his head had been.

Al-Dab'u gave a scream of frustration that turned to a scream of pain as, across the room, Todtman focused the full power of his amulet on him and brought him to his knees.

The Stung Man swivelled towards the kids, more sure on his feet now. A thought formed in Alex's racing mind, simple and undeniable.

He's waking up.

"We have to get out of here!" he shouted to Ren.

"NO!" Todtman yelled. "We must stop him!" He pulled something from around his neck and tossed it high and hard across the room.

Alex reached out instinctively, his palms cupped for a basket catch. The stone beetle hit his palms with a solid thunk, and his hands closed around it. His mother's amulet.

"Try to use the scarab, like this!" said Todtman.

He wrapped his left hand around his own amulet and pushed his right out towards the Stung Man. A humidity monitor lifted off the floor and flew towards the mummy. He swatted it out of the air, and the device landed with a mechanical crunch.

Todtman looked over at Alex. "Your turn."

Alex was sure there was no way he could do what Todtman had, but he turned to face the thing. Holding the scarab in his left hand, he mimicked Todtman and reached out with his right.

Nothing.

Of course not, he thought.

As the Stung Man lurched forward, Alex glanced over at Ren. He recognized the look on her face. Mixed in with the fear was a look he knew far too well, a look he'd seen from classmates and teammates and now his best friend: disappointment.

No! Not any more! He turned back to the Stung Man. He was even closer now. Grasping the scarab, Alex punched out his fist.

A powerful gust of wind rose up and battered the ragged corpse, who stumbled and faltered against it. Alex looked at his hand and his jaw dropped.

Did I do that?

The Stung Man opened his mouth and released a rasping, angry hiss. The fetid smell of the tomb hit Alex and nearly buckled his knees. He put his forearm up over his mouth and coughed into it. He saw Ren bend forward and cover her mouth, doing her best not to retch.

Alex repeated the move more confidently – and another gust of wind slammed into the Stung Man. But the creature leaned into it this time and took a plodding step forward.

"He's too powerful for that now," called Todtman.

"Let's leave," Alex said. "We can lock it in . . . get backup. . ."

Ren darted forward, picked up the shattered humidity monitor, and with a shout of rage, hurled it at the beast. It bounced harmlessly off his rag-wrapped chest.

Ren didn't have a magical amulet, but she wasn't giving up, so neither could he. Alex steeled himself. Still clutching the scarab, he frantically swept the room with his eyes. Through the doorway, he saw the cases housing the Book of the Dead. Somehow, incredibly, he realized he could understand the symbols inside. His mind instantly began to clear, and the rows of hieroglyphs called out to him.

He stared at them.

And as he stared, they began, very faintly, to glow.

Ren gasped.

Todtman looked over.

The Stung Man stopped in his tracks.

Todtman took advantage of the opportunity. Grasping his amulet with one hand, he chopped his other hand down towards the floor.

The Stung Man's left foot kicked sideways into his right, and he staggered on to one knee. As he did, he gazed not at the man who had felled him, but over at the glowing symbols. He shook his head, trying to clear thousands of years of cobwebs.

Alex again felt a glimmer of recognition, almost sympathy. Was there a monster under those rags, or a person? He remembered what he'd read in his mom's book. The Stung Man had started out as a skilled farmer, but in a drought year the pharaoh had taken too large a share of the crop. Weak with malnutrition, the farmer's wife and child had died. Only then did he turn outlaw.

The Stung Man held out his hand, not towards Alex or Todtman, but towards the canopic jars still rattling violently. One after the other, they wooshed towards him.

Fwup! Fwup! Fwup! Fwup!

Lungs, stomach, liver, intestines.

The Stung Man scooped them up under his long arms and let out another ragged hiss, another knee-buckling cloud of stench. Then he turned and stumbled past Ren and Alex, past the glowing symbols. Al-Dab'u climbed to his feet and scurried after him.

A moment later, only the foul smell remained.

Todtman chased after them, but Alex could only stare down at his amulet and then over at the Book of the Dead. The glow was gone, the cases dark.

"Can we leave now?" said Ren. She was shaking badly.

Todtman returned red-faced and out of breath.

"Gone," he said. "I don't know where they went. . ."

He scanned the corners of the room helplessly.

"That guy was the worst guard," said Ren, shaking her head.

Alex couldn't tell if she was joking or just as brain-fried as him. He stopped midway through the room and stared at the empty sarcophagus. The others stopped, too.

Alex wanted to say something about it, but he didn't have the energy. As the three of them stood there looking, the lights clicked back on. All over the museum, alarms went off like distant fireworks.

"That's better," said Todtman.

Alex could only nod. He heard footsteps and turned towards the door in time to see Oscar and another guard burst in.

"What happened?" said Oscar.

Alex had no idea how to answer that. But Todtman did.

"It was another robbery," he said. "They got the Stung Man, I'm afraid."

16

THE BOOK CLUB

Alex and Ren were seated in Todtman's office, watching silently as Todtman took out a bottle of headache pills and popped two in his mouth.

Alex knew what that was like – he could practically taste the gritty chalk of the dissolving tablets. He looked down at his amulet and then over at Ren. She was still breathing hard, her hands shaking slightly.

He listened to the sound of his pulse in his head. The beats were hard and fast, and every one sounded like a single word to him: *Mom*.

It was bad enough before, he thought.

It was bad enough when he thought his mom had been kidnapped.

Before he knew the smell of the crypt.

Before he knew that the dead could wake.

There was something much larger going on. And somehow his mother was a part of it. The Spells were gone but her scarab was here, her scarab had powers—

He needed answers.

"Who are you?" he asked Todtman.

Todtman swallowed the pills and pointed to the little sign on his desk: DR ERNST TODTMAN.

"Yeah, but who are you *really*?" Ren said. Her eyes were still wide with shock and fear, but Alex could see her fight to push all that aside and focus. He felt a rush of gratitude.

"I can assure you that is my real name," said Todtman. His tone was measured, but Alex knew he wasn't unaffected by what had just happened. Ren's hands weren't the only ones that were shaking.

"I am associate director of the Neues Museum in Berlin," Todtman continued, his accent colouring his words just slightly. "I am an Egyptologist and a colleague of your mother's – and a friend. We are members of a sort of . . . there is a word for it in German, but I do not think there is quite the right one in English. A sort of . . . group, perhaps?"

"A secret society?" said Ren, leaning forward.

"Mmmmm, more like . . . a professional organization. Some call us the Keepers. We are scholars, mostly. We help each other in our studies, share our findings – sometimes we read the same book."

"You're . . . *a book club*?" said Ren.

Todtman smiled. Alex had seen that smile before: The heavy flesh of his cheeks creased and lifted, the already buggy eyes opened even wider. It had seemed sinister to him when he first met Todtman, but now it seemed less frog-like and more friendly.

"You had his mom's beetle thing," Ren accused.

Alex felt a flash of guilt. He should have said that.

"She left the amulet for me," said Todtman with a shrug. "At least that's what I think. It was found in a case in the new exhibition. A loose piece, out of place . . . she had to know it would be brought to me."

"Wait," said Alex, determined to get his head around it all. "Is anyone going to talk about the crazy undead mummy that just tried to *eat our souls*?"

"We're getting to that," protested Ren. "We have

to start with things I can understand or my head is going to explode, all right?"

"All right," he said. He could hear the strain in Ren's voice and see the confusion in her eyes. Her world had just turned upside down.

This was easier for him. He'd been raised on stories of ancient Egypt and ancient magic. He just had to accept that those stories were true – and how could he deny that now? He tried to come up with a question that wasn't too head-explode-y. "The guard in the mask. You called him Al-Dab'u? And he could do things – we could all do things. . ."

"Not all of us," said Ren, more to herself.

Todtman considered the question.

"Yes, let's start with him. Not a guard, not really – though he had me fooled. He works for an organization out of Egypt, very powerful," said Todtman. "They call him Al-Dab'u – the Hyena. I'm sure you can see why."

Ren nodded. One clear connection, one answer. Todtman continued.

"And the organization, well, I'm afraid they *are* a secret society. They are called The Order, at least that's how you'd say it in English. In Egypt, people think of The Order like the mafia in Italy, or the yakuza in Japan: powerful, violent and with strange traditions. And like those organizations, this one is very old. But they are not truly like the others."

"Why not?" said Ren. "We have the mafia here, too, by the way."

Todtman tipped his head, thanking her for the information. "Because they are a death cult," he said. "The mafia, here or there, the yakuza; they exist for the money, the power. The Order serves a man who has been dead for thousands of years. They'd been hunting for the Lost Spells, because their ultimate goal is to bring him back."

"The Stung Man?" said Alex.

"No, but like him."

"A Death Walker?" said Alex.

"How do you know about the Death Walkers?" said Todtman, surprised. "But yes, another Death Walker."

"Think I read one of your books. . ."

"Wait, there's a book?" said Ren, sitting up straighter. "Can I read it?"

Alex was about to answer when Todtman held up one finger.

"What?" said Alex, eager for another revelation.

Todtman lowered his finger and pointed it at the door. As he did, there was a loud knock.

"I'll have to get that, I'm afraid," said Todtman. "It's the police."

"Just one minute, please!" he called towards the door.

"Obviously, we have much more to discuss," he said, lowering his voice again.

"Obviously," echoed Ren, shooting him a look that said, *And don't you forget it*.

"Yeah, like what does this have to do with my mom?" said Alex, hating that his voice broke. "And the amulets? And—"

"I know this is difficult," said Todtman, "but right now, the police will want to talk to us. And you need to listen to me carefully."

"You want to tell us what to say?" said Ren.

"You could put it that way, but please understand. These people – that *creature* – there is nothing the police can do. Guns, prisons, juries. . . They are no obstacles to him. And if we were to say what we saw here tonight, what we did. . ."

"We'd be the ones who'd get locked up," said Ren.

"'Mass psychosis,'" said Alex.

"At the very least, it would get in the way

of what we need to do. And we want the same thing."

"To stop them?" said Alex.

"Yes, and to find what was taken."

"And my *mom*."

"Of course."

Alex looked him in the eyes, and he thought he saw understanding there. This man had said he was his mom's friend.

"You called my mom? Before she left?"

"A friend of ours was hurt, in Cairo. She was upset. We both were."

Alex nodded. He decided to believe him. What choice did he have?

Another knock on the door, louder this time. Todtman and Alex both looked at Ren. She nodded, too. "OK."

"I'll have to unlock that," said Todtman, looking at the door as if it were a thousand miles away. He glanced down at his own amulet – in the shape of a bird, Alex noticed – then over at the bottle of headache pills. He pushed back his chair. "I think I'll do it the old-fashioned way."

As Todtman got up and walked past them, Ren leaned over to Alex. She wasn't shaking any more.

"Do you believe this?" she whispered.

"What part?" he whispered back.

"They've got a death cult," she said as the door opened behind them. "And we've got a book club."

17

AMULET

And after all of that, Alex had to head back across town – and hope no one had pulled that ladder back up. "I don't think they'll come after you," Todtman had said by way of goodbye. "Not right away. But maybe you should take a taxi."

Not exactly comforting. Still, Alex needed some time to himself to process all this, and he was still exploring the limits of his new-found strength, so he decided to walk home. He made his way slowly through Central Park, sticking to the well-lit main roads and keeping a close eye on the shifting shadows around him. Mostly, though, he thought about his mom. She felt both closer now and further away. *This organization, The Order, must have her,* he thought. *The Order must have taken the Lost Spells and my mom.* Alex considered Todtman: He was definitely strange, but he'd saved his life and Ren's, too. *Could he help me save my mom?*

Alex held his hand out in front of him to see if it was still shaking. Just a little. He reached up with it and wiped away the tears that were beginning to well up in his eyes. He was alone now, and he was a mess. He needed a plan – or something he could do—

He took the familiar amulet out from under his shirt and looked at it for a few steps. It was beautiful but also plain, just polished stone and refined copper. It was a winged beetle, carved thousands of years ago – and it could do things. He wasn't sure exactly what, but there was no doubt it was special.

Mom must have known, he thought. *Why didn't she tell me?* She'd always protected him, he knew that, but had she always kept him in the dark, too? He shook the thought out of his head and felt the amulet's silver chain scratch against his neck. He reached up for it again. "All right, little beetle," he said softly, "let's see what you can do."

He looked around him, in front and behind, and waited for a lone jogger to pass. He closed his left hand around the scarab, a sense of anticipation, of something about to happen, tingling through him. His mind raced and his pulse revved. He took the last of the ebbing adrenaline inside his body and focused it.

Alex pushed his right hand out towards the top of a nearby tree, thick with fat green summer leaves. A leaf began to whip. Then the whole branch started to sway. He tightened his grip and pointed his fingers, and the leaves began to tear free and fly off into the softly glowing New York night, and it was so unbelievable that Alex couldn't help but laugh at the strangeness of it. He released the amulet and looked at his hand. *Yep*, he thought, *that really happened*.

He kept walking and breathed deeply. He had a lot of practice with that. His pulse began to slow; his nerves began to calm. He missed the rush before it was even fully gone. A single word formed in his racing mind: *dangerous*. After a lifetime of caution, he kind of liked the sound of that.

What else could it do? Todtman had done something to Al-Dab'u's mind.

"Get out of my head"? Isn't that what he'd said? Is that how he beat him? Another jogger passed. Alex held the scarab and touched his other hand to his temple. He looked at the jogger, her ponytail swinging left-right, left-right as she ran. *Turn around*, he thought. *TURN AROUND*. Nothing. *Hop!* he tried. *Jump!* Nothing. She turned the corner and was gone.

Either his amulet didn't work that way, or he wasn't doing it right. And now his head was starting to hurt, too. The rush he liked. The headache, not so much. He let go of the amulet and walked on in silence towards his aunt and uncle's apartment. The darkness was full of eerie rustlings, but Alex was too exhausted to care.

As he approached the west side of the park, he saw a group of people clustered near a street light by the entrance. They were looking down at something on the ground. It took Alex a moment to realize it was a person. He hurried over, taking out his cell phone as he ran.

"What's wrong with her?" said a man in a Yankees cap.

"She says she was bitten," said an old lady holding a very small dog.

"Bitten?" said the man.

"Look at her leg," said a younger woman.

Alex crowded in. It was the jogger from before. He had a flash of panic: *Did I do that?* But when he saw the wound, he knew he hadn't. There was a swollen red circle just above her ankle. The jogger had her eyes closed and her teeth clenched.

"Are there any snakes in the park?" said the man as they waited for the ambulance.

The old woman gasped. "I've never seen one here!" she said, holding her little dog tighter.

Alex scanned the ground one last time and caught a sudden jitter of movement at the edge of the street light's glow.

Just a quick glimpse of a small, spiky shadow.

Alex would've had no idea what it was.

If he hadn't seen the stinger.

18

SCORPIONS

Alex and Ren met across the street from the museum the next morning and waited for Todtman. "Hey, did you bring that Death Walkers book?" said Ren.

"Couldn't find it," said Alex. "I could've sworn I had it by the window, but it wasn't there."

"You ask your aunt and uncle?"

"Said they hadn't seen it."

"What about your cousin?"

"Luke's not much of a reader."

"Oh, wait, here comes Todtman."

He walked up carrying an extremely large coffee in one hand and a newspaper under one arm. "Good morning," he said. "Let's walk."

He headed towards Central Park, and Alex and Ren tagged along on either side.

"We should, uh, watch our step in here," said Alex, eyeing the ground as they entered the park.

"Indeed," said Todtman. "There's something I want to show you. You both have strong stomachs, I hope."

Alex and Ren glanced over at each other: *strong stomachs?*

"And you've both seen the news?"

Todtman flashed the front page at them. The headline: "Stung Man Sprung from Cursed Exhibit."

"They didn't mention us by name," said Ren. "But they mentioned you."

"Did you get in trouble?" asked Alex.

"Not exactly," Todtman said cryptically, dropping the paper in a trash can without breaking stride.

They hooked a right and headed deeper into the park.

Ren tested the water with a softball question. "So what's your deal anyway?" she asked Todtman. "Why Egypt? Why not. . ."

"Please don't say World War II," he said, not unkindly. Alex looked around to see if anyone was following them or listening in. Todtman continued: "Egypt has been a passion of mine since I was young – younger than you two. I took a trip when I was eight."

"It's not as far from Germany," volunteered Ren.

"True, but still far. My family was neither rich nor poor, and the trip was a big event. My father had got a bonus, I believe. In any case, eight years old. I'd never seen anything more impressive than a well-made cuckoo clock, and here were pyramids as high as skyscrapers. We floated down the Nile and our guides took us down into a tomb. The sarcophagus was still inside. I was done for. Hooked."

Alex knew the feeling, but they hadn't come here to talk about vacations. "Shouldn't we go someplace private?" he said, waving his hand at the park's famous scenery.

"But this is very private today, isn't it?" said Todtman.

Alex looked again. The park should've been packed on a summer day like this, but the trails were mostly empty. He didn't see a single jogger. He remembered the scene last night, the face twisted in pain. He could understand that. But what about the tourists, the dog-walkers. . .

He heard a rustling just off the path and jumped away.

"There are scorpions here," he said.

It sounded silly in the daylight, but he knew what he'd seen. And the others weren't exactly laughing.

"They're all over the city," said Ren. "Didn't you read any of the other stories?"

Alex shook his head. Ren gave him a disapproving look and turned towards Todtman. "The news says it's because of people releasing 'exotic pets' and climate change."

Todtman considered that for a moment as they walked. "When faced with the impossible, people will always cling to what they know," he said.

This time Alex gave Ren a look. She ignored it.

"Was that a real mummy?" she asked. No more softball questions.

"Quite real," said Todtman.

"He didn't look like one," she countered.

"True, his life force has returned to his body."

A flash of recognition nearly stopped Alex in his tracks.

"How is that possible?" said Ren, but Alex could

hear the fight leaving her voice. She'd seen the same thing he had, and it wasn't some nut job in gauze.

"No, my turn," said Alex. "What are, um, what about the amulets?"

Todtman had been expecting that one: "We only know of a handful with these kinds of powers, though there could be more. Mine is in the shape of a falcon, the symbol of the watcher."

"Because of their eyesight," said Ren.

"Yes," said Todtman, "and their range."

"Mine, well, my mom's, it's a scarab," said Alex.

"Yes, the returner, a symbol of rebirth and regeneration."

Another flash of recognition. Ren snuck in a question as Alex began to put the pieces together. "How did you find them?"

Todtman cocked his head to consider. "We think they found us. Alex's mother was the first. She found the scarab on a dig near Sudan. I found mine in a market bazaar."

"So anyone could have. . ."

"I don't think so. They only seem to work for one person – one person at a time, at least. It's like they put themselves in our path. Hundreds of people must have picked mine up and felt nothing, no spark of recognition. And I felt none with the scarab."

"And they each do different things, don't they?" Alex asked.

Todtman fixed Alex with his bugged-out eyes and smiled. "You understand, then. I thought you might, once I saw you use the scarab. Yes, all of them can do certain things. Move small objects, and so on, but mine, well, I can see things quite clearly sometimes. When the power went out, I knew to go straight to the sarcophagus. I can also control people to an extent. A watcher can also be a boss, of course, an overseer. But the scarab, it's much more powerful."

"I can do, like, a wind thing," said Alex.

"The wind that comes before the rain," said Todtman. "Another kind of rebirth – but the scarab can do much more than that. It's the reason we're all here, isn't it?"

"Wait, what do you mean?" said Ren.

Alex turned the words over. The next piece of the puzzle clicked into place, and everything in him went cold. "The reason I'm still here. . ." he said.

Ren looked from Todtman to Alex and back. "Tell me!" she said as they took another turn, heading deeper into the park. They were far from the street now, and the trees seemed to close in around them.

"In the hospital, my mom. . ." He turned to Todtman. "I thought I dreamed that, but. . ." He almost couldn't say it. "She used the amulet, didn't she?"

"She used the Lost Spells," he said. "I warned her not to – no offence to you, Alex – but she was desperate. It seems the scarab can activate the Book of the Dead. I believe we saw that last night, too. I think that's what spooked the Stung Man. It can give the old spells their power back. And the Book of the Dead is *very* powerful, whether it's moving someone towards the afterlife – or, in the case of the Lost Spells, bringing them out of it."

Alex remembered the ancient text, glowing faintly. His head reeled at the implications. "Mom brought me back," he whispered. "Reattached my life force."

"The returner," said Todtman.

"But not just me. . ."

A new possibility opened up for Alex. He felt like he was falling down a well, waiting to hit bottom.

"The door to the afterlife was opened." Todtman

paused and looked down. "I told her there was a risk."

"So now there's a *door* to the afterlife?" said Ren, exasperated.

Todtman turned to her, his eyebrows high with surprise. "Yes, of course. There are many."

"And what got out?" asked Alex. "Of the doors?"

"Whatever was waiting, it seems. That includes the Stung Man, of course. We don't know who else. . . The Death Walkers were waiting – how many of them got out, though? It could be any of them; it could be all of them. They are certainly all quite dangerous. Men and women whose hearts were heavy with evil thousands of years ago – well, I doubt they've got nicer with time."

Alex had one last flash of recognition, but this one was more like a lightning bolt. He reached the bottom of the well. He crashed down. "This is all my fault. . ."

He looked up at Todtman, hoping he would say something reassuring, tell Alex he'd completely misunderstood.

But Todtman said nothing, just kept walking.

Alex struggled to find words – *sorry*, maybe, though *sorry* didn't remotely cut it – but his throat was clamped shut. All this because of him. All this so he could live. The Stung Man with his wet, malevolent eyes, the little mummy who couldn't sleep. His mom, missing. And all because of him.

Ren looked from Alex to Todtman and opened her mouth, but seemed to think better of it. Instead, she took a step closer to Alex and simply walked next to him. Emotional Support Position.

The group took one final turn. They were near the centre of the park now. They were alone in a park that was too empty, too quiet. They stuck to the centre of the path.

"So why do they need Alex's mom?" Ren finally said, a few steps later. "I mean, *if* all this is true."

"Perhaps because they know she knows how to use the Spells," said Todtman. "Though she would need the amulet. I'm not sure they've made that connection yet."

Alex looked at him. *Did that put her in less danger, or more?* Todtman's expression gave nothing away.

"I'm grounded, you know?" said Ren. "My parents just think it was a robbery last night, but still."

Alex realized she was talking just to talk now, that she needed to hear the sound of a human voice in this empty place.

"I mean, I know I don't *seem* grounded, but they don't really check. . ."

"We're almost there," interrupted Todtman. "You can smell it now."

Alex breathed in through his nose. It was a rank smell, not overpowering yet, but not good.

They were walking up a small hill, approaching the top.

"Smells like wet dog," said Ren.

They reached the top of the little hill and looked down.

"No," said Todtman. "It smells like death."

They gazed down on the park's main sanitation substation. Workers in green coveralls and white masks were standing on a platform and shovelling dead animals into a massive metal shipping container. Alex saw squirrels and pigeons by the shovelful, along with some stray cats and even ducks and geese.

So many of them, tossed on to the pile like heavy, wet pillows.

The scorpions, Alex thought.

"I have to include you in this now, Alex," said Todtman softly. "I didn't want to, but I cannot use the scarab and I think it is the key. I need you both to see how big this is. And how dangerous. This" – he gestured to the gruesome scene in front of them – "is just the beginning. The Order has always been powerful, but now the Death Walkers are returning, as the cult had long hoped they would. They are working together, and that is a very dangerous combination."

Dangerous, thought Alex. *There's that word again.*

But it didn't matter.

"It's my mom," he said with a sharp nod of his head. "And my fault. I'm in."

Todtman regarded Ren solemnly. "Ren, you are a smart girl, and I suppose you can make up your own mind, but I would prefer it if you were not involved."

They were all quiet for a while, the scrape of shovels the only thing to break the silence.

Ren spoke first.

"You don't want me 'involved'?" she asked. Her voice was quiet, but Alex recognized the fierce look on her face.

"No."

"Well, tough," she said. "Alex is my best friend. And his mom is my third-favourite parent."

Todtman's expression remained flat, unmoved.

"Just the same," he said, "I see no reason to endanger your life, too."

"Friends stick together," Ren said. "It's non-negotiable."

Alex felt a huge rush of gratitude. He didn't want Ren mixed up in this mess, but he didn't know how he could do this without her.

"And anyway," she said, "I know where the Stung Man and Al-Dab'u went."

Now Todtman's expression changed. It was pure surprise.

"Where they went?" said Todtman.

"Yeah, how they got away from you at the museum, with the Stung Man still moving so slowly. . ."

"How?" said Todtman.

"I'll tell you," she said as they turned and began the walk back to Fifth Avenue. "But it smells even worse than this place."

Alex didn't care what it smelled like. He wasn't the logical list maker that Ren was, but he'd figured something out in his little bedroom office the night before, a pure logic equation that kept running through his mind:

The Order has Mom. If I find Al-Dab'u and the Stung Man, I find Mom.

He looked over at Ren, but she didn't notice. Her hands were balled into fists, and he knew her mind was grinding away at all this.

Their mission had changed, but he still had exactly the right partner.

19

DIRTY WORK

"You look ridiculous," Alex said to Ren.

They had just dropped through a drain in the floor of the Met's sub-basement and were in an old sewer tunnel. Ren had rubber boots on her feet, a mask on her face, and a white plastic suit everywhere else. The suit was way too big for her, so the sleeves and legs were bunched up with thick rubber bands. All of the gear had come from Todtman, courtesy of a trip to the Home Depot on Fifty-Ninth.

"I guess sewer suits don't come in petite sizes,"

she said, swinging a large flashlight back and forth in front of her. The beam lit a stream of dark, soup-thick water passing by below them. The masks were designed to filter out things like fibreglass insulation and cement dust, but did little for the smell.

"I think these suits are supposed to be for painting," said Alex.

"This place could use a good paint job," said Ren as she swung her flashlight across the mouldy, filth-caked top of the old sewer tunnel.

"How did you know this connected to the museum, anyway?" said Alex.

"My dad mentioned it once: 'drainage subbasement'. I'd been thinking about how the two of them managed to just disappear. How could the Stung Man have outrun Todtman? Plus there were guards at all the exits, because of the blackout. They couldn't just magically disappear – I think – so, where could they have gone?" She swung her flashlight around again. "No guards here."

Alex managed a nervous laugh. He was at least as scared as he was grossed out, and the chatter helped. *Remember why you're here*, he told himself. *Remember the mission.* If Al-Dab'u and the Stung

Man really exited this way, then they needed to figure out where they went. He fingered his amulet to calm his nerves a little.

Ren was holding her flashlight in her left hand and wielding a small crowbar in her right. He wasn't sure how much good that would do. . .

Alex swept his flashlight in front of him and tried to find a clear spot to put his foot down. They were walking along a thin ledge, just above the slow-flowing sludge. He stopped for a moment to check their printout of the Upper East Side sewer system with the flashlight.

"We are totally doing Todtman's dirty work," said Ren.

"I'm not sure I'd want to be him at the museum today, either," said Alex.

"This is still tougher," said Ren, stomping her boot down in the muck to make her point. "Not many people could do this."

Alex didn't disagree with either statement, but he didn't really see where she was going with it. "OK," he said.

"Like, do you think Jesse could do this?"

"Jesse Blatz?"

"Yeah, just for example."

"You need to get over that kid. You're just as smart as him."

"I'm maybe sixty per cent as smart as him," she said and whacked at the air with her crowbar. "Just answer the question."

"Do I think he could do this?"

"Yeah."

"Walk through toilet water? Probably."

"I don't mean that. I mean, I don't know, get chased by a mummy and then chase it back."

"Then, no. I don't think he could do this."

Ren's white mask bobbed up and down in an emphatic nod. "I don't, either."

Alex took a few more steps through the turgid muck. "He's too smart to."

They both chuckled. It echoed slightly in the tunnel and they nervously swung their flashlights from side to side in the darkness.

The ledge narrowed and Alex gave up on it and stepped off so he was up to his ankles in a slowly flowing, stew-thick stream. They trudged on quietly for a while. It was quiet except for the squelching of their feet. It was horrible down here, but it was just the two of them – at least he hoped it was. He felt like he could say anything. And hadn't Ren just done that?

"Hey, Ren?"

"Yeah?"

"Do you think this. . ." He took a few more steps. "Never mind."

"What?"

"OK. Well. Do *you* think this is all my fault?"

"No way! Don't be dumb," she said – and then very quickly changed the subject. "Anyway, we have to concentrate. Keep your eyes open."

"What exactly are we looking for? It's not like they would've left footprints."

This time he stomped his foot to make his point.

"Look for scraps of cloth," said Ren. "That thing's, like, mummy garb didn't look too secure."

Alex stopped to check the sewer map again and something solid bumped into his boot. He swung his flashlight around, but whatever it was had already drifted downstream. A few minutes later, something else floated by. This time, he got his flashlight on it. It was a dead rat. "Gross," he said.

"I saw one of those, too," Ren called from up on the ledge.

After another ten minutes of trudging straight ahead, they came to a T-shaped junction in the pipes. Alex located it on the map. "Which way?" he said.

Both passages smelled terrible. They swept their flashlights in one direction: nothing. Then the other: "Is that another rat?" said Ren.

It was. And this one was up out of the water, lying dead on its side on the narrow walking ledge. Ren headed towards it.

"I guess we're going this way," said Alex, following along.

Ren bent down over the dead rodent, and Alex leaned over her shoulder for a look. "Does it seem weird that we haven't seen any *live* rats down here?" he said.

"I think I know why," said Ren, holding her flashlight closer to the carcass. "See that?"

Alex saw. "It's a *sting*."

"Well," said Ren, "not exactly a footprint, but. . ."

They followed the trail of dead rats for what felt like five miles – and smelled like fifty. Every movement and every sound made them jump. It wasn't just the certainty of dead rats and the possibility of live scorpions that had them on edge. They were alone, in the dark. And the Stung Man could be anywhere.

Todtman was sure he would be long gone, that the sewer was "a route and not a destination". But Todtman wasn't there.

As Alex walked, he frequently had to stoop down to avoid bumping his head. Ren, not so much. Finally, the passage began to slope slightly upwards. The floors got drier and pipes ceased to pour filth in on them. There were even occasional slivers of daylight filtering in from above. It all came to a dead end at a battered concrete wall.

Alex smacked the wall. He'd been so sure they were going to find something.

They hadn't seen a dead rat for a while now and seemed to have run out of leads. Alex checked the map again. "I think maybe we're near Lexington Avenue," he said.

Ren inched her flashlight beam slowly across the concrete, and that's when they saw it: a dark, narrow gash that didn't catch the light. There was a vertical gap in the wall.

Alex walked over to it, took a deep breath, and ducked his head through.

"See anything?" said Ren.

"It looks like another tunnel, but it's too dark to tell."

He stood still.

"Wait. . . I think I *feel* something."

"I feel it, too," confirmed Ren. "It's getting stronger."

It started as a faint rumbling – just a tickle in the soles of Alex's boots – but it quickly grew strong enough to rattle his teeth. For a few seconds, Alex was afraid it was an earthquake. *I do NOT want to die down here,* he thought. Then he saw a bright round light in the distance and yanked his head back through the gap as it approached.

He had to shout to be heard over the noise: "It's the subway!"

The rumbling reached a crescendo as the train whipped by on the other side. They could see the lights and hear the wind from the subway cars.

As soon as it passed by, Ren rushed forward and stuck her head through the gap. It was wide enough that she could have squeezed through it if she wanted.

"What was it?" asked Alex.

She pulled her head back in: "The 4 train. Downtown express. We're under Lexington Avenue!"

Alex felt like hitting the wall again – maybe

punching it this time. "If they got into the subway tunnels, they could be anywhere now."

Ren kept quiet. She didn't have an answer to that.

They had to trudge back through the sewer, back through dead rats and unspeakably gross sludge, to get to the closest manhole. They marched together in silence. Ren coughed because of the smell every once in a while, and Alex's mind was on his mother. Eventually, they spotted the narrow steel rungs of the little ladder. Alex went up first with the crowbar. It was the first time he'd really tested his new strength.

His muscles began burning almost immediately, unaccustomed to the effort. He wanted to take a break, but didn't want Ren to see him fail. He put all his weight into one big push, and the heavy lid finally popped loose.

Timing the traffic was tougher, and Alex was too impatient to wait. He'd been down there long enough. He listened for the first break in traffic and then muscled the manhole cover aside.

"Wait!" called Ren, a few rungs below.

Alex popped his head out to look and a taxi nearly whack-a-moled him. He ducked down and reached up to see if his head was still there. He tried again:

all clear. He scrambled up the little ladder, then stood there with his hand out in a stop sign.

There was only so official a twelve-year-old was going to look in late-afternoon traffic, but the suit and mask helped. Ren scrambled up after him, then they pushed and kicked the lid back in place and sprinted to the kerb. A sidewalk full of shoppers stared at them. They were so relieved to be back in the daylight that they barely noticed.

"Gas leak," said Ren matter-of-factly. "Everything's OK now, though."

They hurried around the corner and peeled off their filth-splattered plastic suits. Ren took the opportunity to scold Alex about the taxi. "You took a lot of dumb chances back there," she said. "Wading through that sludge – what if you'd stepped on something sharp? And you almost lost your head rushing into traffic."

Alex shrugged. He was done with being careful about every little move. He took out his phone. "We think they went into the subway tunnels," he said when Todtman picked up. "Because that's where the trail leads. And also because we really, really don't want to go back into the sewer."

*

Alex's aunt and uncle still weren't home when he got back to the apartment that evening. The door to Luke's room was open, and Alex ducked his head in. The walls were covered in posters. Alex was expecting football and baseball, but what he saw was mostly track and a lot of Olympic rings. Luke was on a mat on the floor doing yoga. Alex decided not to comment. Because: muscles. "Olympics, huh?" he said instead.

"That's the plan," said Luke, continuing to stare at the ceiling, as the pose required.

"What, like, event?" Alex was in shaky territory here. There were only a few events he really knew about.

"Decathlon."

Alex did, however, speak more ancient Greek than most kids. "That means ten – ten events?"

Luke changed positions. If Alex had to give this one a name, he'd call it Improbable Crab pose. "Yeah, ten events," said Luke, "but I got a strategy. If I get really good at one of them, I can just switch and concentrate on that. It's called *specialization*."

Luke pronounced the word like it was a fancy French dessert.

"That's a lot of work," said Alex.

"I like the work," said Luke, his muscles beginning to tremble with the strain of the pose. "Problem is it's expensive. Camps, coaches, travel. 'Rents kind of aren't having it." Luke collapsed on to the mat and wiped the sweat from his face with his forearm. He looked over and flashed a quick, unhappy smile. "Say I should just play football."

Alex gave him his best *I hear ya, man* headshake, but what he was really thinking about was his struggle with the manhole cover and how he still got winded so quickly. "Hey, Luke," he said, "think you could show me some of those poses sometime?"

"Sure thing, little man," he said. Alex wished he wouldn't call him that. Luke was a good six inches taller than him but only a year and a half older.

Alex knew he needed to shower – and probably shower again – but he was eager to get back to his little room. He needed to practise with the amulet. He told himself that even if they hadn't found the Stung Man today, they would eventually. That would mean another confrontation – on enemy turf this time.

He closed his door and poured a small bag of glass marbles out on to the desk. He had to start somewhere, and he heard Todtman's words from that first night: *"All of them can do certain things. Move small objects, and so on."*

It took him a while, but soon he could roll a marble across the desk and back again. Even after all he'd seen, it was still amazing to feel his pulse rev and see the little blue orb start to roll on its own, and then to change directions. His whole life he could barely move his own body – now he could do things even Luke's Olympians couldn't.

He grasped the amulet tighter and tried for two at once. For a second it worked, but then a small crack appeared in the second one and – *prakk!* – it fractured all the way through. Alex looked back at the first one, still clutching the amulet tightly. It shot straight forward, pinged against the wall, and dropped down behind the desk.

The marbles weren't the only casualty. He released the amulet and shook out his hand. The wings had pressed deep crescents into his skin, and now his head hurt. He put the remaining marbles back in the bag.

His head cleared after dinner, and he practised some more. He couldn't quite open and close the window, but he could lock and unlock it. He was getting better, but before long his headache was back. *Is it worse this time?* he wondered as he went to the bathroom to look for aspirin. He reached for the handle of the medicine cabinet.

He missed.

He squinted at the little handle.

He saw two of them.

It was worse. Definitely worse.

He took three aspirin. He saw six.

Before bed, he decided to use the scarab for one more thing. He wanted to feel that electric quickening one more time. And the urge to see if he could set the alarm clock was irresistible.

Why didn't Mom tell me about this? he wondered as he stared at the little buttons. He'd been picking at the question like a scab. He couldn't let it go. *She wore it every day, so why did she leave it behind?* He managed to change the hour and was working on the minutes when he was blindsided by a new possibility: *Did she know she wasn't coming back?* An ugly spatter of words snuck up on him, as if whispered into his ear: *He needs to feed.* There was a thick crunch from the alarm clock and the numbers blinked out.

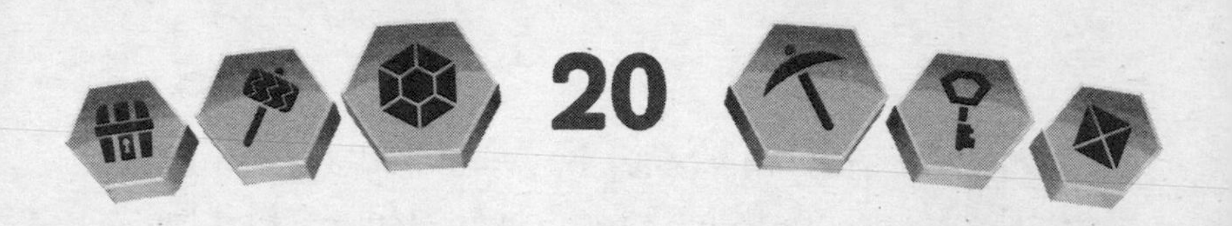

TRACKING THE ENEMY

Alex was sitting in the living room, resting his throbbing head on his arm. Another beautiful summer day, and another feeling of overwhelming helplessness.

“Enjoy the sun!” Adele said loudly as she passed by Alex.

“Some fresh air will take that frown off your face,” added his uncle Gerry.

Alex looked at them. *(A) you don't know me at all*, he thought. *And (B) no it won't.*

My mom is still missing!

He didn't say any of that, though, just told them to have a good time at the farmers' market and picked up their discarded *Post*. He wondered if his mom's subscription to the *Times* was piling up outside their door.

The lead story caught his attention immediately. The chaos at the museum had been knocked out of the top spot by a strange story about stolen stones. And not small stones: One of the famous lion statues had been stolen from in front of the New York Public Library overnight. One of the columns had disappeared from the old Union Square Savings Bank building, too. A few stone blocks had even been swiped from the base of the Brooklyn Bridge.

The last one was the worst and had its own little story. "Scared to Death?" read the headline. A guard had been found dead near the bridge. The police suspected a heart attack since there wasn't a mark on him. Alex thought of Oscar and the rest of the guards at the Met. He considered them friends.

What if something happens to one of them?

What if it's because of me?

He shook his head hard and the paper rattled

in his hands, but he read on. The stone blocks from the bridge were huge and weighed tons. They reminded him of the blocks used to construct the Great Pyramid: 2.5 tons each.

Like the other thefts, this one had involved a bogus construction project, a flatbed truck, and surprisingly few witnesses. He looked at the picture: massive stones removed like LEGO blocks. He grabbed his phone and texted Ren.

An hour later, he met her outside the museum. "You still grounded?" he said.

"No," she said, "they think I've suffered enough."

Todtman let them in the staff entrance. Once they reached his office, he pointed to a box of doughnuts in the corner. "For yesterday," he said.

Alex perused the selection. Two sugar-covered jelly doughnuts for four hours in the sewer seemed about right to him. Ren chose a chocolate glazed. "These are so bad for your teeth!" she said between large bites.

Then they got down to business. Todtman – who'd surprised them both by opting for a doughnut with pink sprinkles – spread a map of the city out on his desk. "You've seen the news, yes?" he said.

"Before we talk about the subway, let's look at what happened last night."

Ren and Alex crowded around as he smoothed out the map and picked up a yellow highlighter. He made a circle. "This is Forty-Second Street, the public library," he said.

"The lion," said Alex.

Another circle. "This is Union Square," said Todtman.

"The column," said Ren.

A third circle. "Brooklyn Bridge," they all said.

"Connected to our problem, I think," said Todtman.

"Ancient Egypt and big stones." Alex nodded. "Like peanut butter and chocolate."

Todtman straightened up. "Now, let's talk about the subway," he said. "Tell me what you found."

Ren smiled. "We're already talking about it."

She held out her hand for the highlighter. Todtman passed it to her as if he were handing a scalpel to a surgeon. She drew a line. It started near the museum, swooped downtown, past the library, through Union Square, down to the Brooklyn Bridge.

"The downtown express," she said.

The others leaned in for a closer look.

"I think you've earned another doughnut," said Todtman, smiling.

"No thanks," said Ren. "But I'll tell you something else."

"Yes?"

"There are abandoned stations down there. Did an extra-credit report on them once."

Once again, Alex knew she was right. Underground chambers and mummies . . . like ketchup and fries.

"We're going there, aren't we?" he said.

"How else will we know if we're right?" said Todtman with his froggy smile.

Alex thought about it. An undead thief and a fanatical dog-headed mafioso camped out in an abandoned subway station: less smelly than the sewers but way more scary. "Should we, uh, should we not have thrown away those flashlights? They were pretty gross."

"Alex dropped his," Ren volunteered.

"I don't think they will be hard to replace," said Todtman. "But we will need to take something else with us. And it is *quite* irreplaceable."

He took a step to the side and opened the top

drawer of his desk. Ren peeked over. "Whoa," she said. "What're we gonna do with those?"

Alex felt the amulet getting warm against his chest.

"Doors swing both ways, after all," said Todtman. "And I think we might be able to put our problem to rest."

Alex would never have guessed that public transportation would be so convenient for chasing evil. They took the downtown express to the Brooklyn Bridge–City Hall stop. It was just a short distance from the old Worth Street station, which had been abandoned for decades but was still on the old maps. And the Met was full of old maps.

"We should go to the end of the platform," said Todtman, walking briskly in front of them.

Ren nodded, then held out her hand so Alex could see. It was shaking.

"We will have to wait until there are no trains coming," said Todtman.

"But people will see us climb down," said Alex.

"Probably not," said Todtman, and gave Alex an awkward wink. He was wearing his amulet outside his shirt now, and it bounced with each step. Alex looked at it. It was beautiful: a bright blue falcon with wings outstretched, edged in gold, and two glittering gems for eyes. The watcher.

"Oh, right," said Alex. He fished his own amulet out from under his T-shirt.

They walked to the end of the platform – the furthest point from where the next train would arrive. Todtman wrapped his hand around his amulet. A moment later, everyone in the station started to peer down the tracks in the opposite direction. Todtman gestured for them to get moving. Ren carefully lowered herself down on to the tracks. The climb down was close to four feet – almost as tall as her – and she stumbled a bit at the bottom. She got a long black smudge on her new blue shirt.

"Ah, man," she said.

"Don't worry about your shirt," said Alex.

"Says the guy wearing jewellery."

"It's not!" Alex protested. Then he squatted down, put one hand on the platform edge for balance, and jumped down on to the tracks.

"Be careful!" whispered Todtman.

His tone reminded Alex of the doctors. *I'm not that kid any more*, he thought.

Ren glared at him. He could see what she was thinking: *Another dumb risk*. "Well, watch out for the third rail, anyway," she said. "If you touch that thing, you're barbecue."

"Hurry now," said Todtman, completing his own climb down on to the tracks.

Surprisingly nimble for an old guy, thought Alex.

Todtman took the lead as they hustled into the dark mouth of the tunnel and out of sight. "Backpack, please," he said after a few more steps.

Alex swung it off his back and unzipped it. "Why am I the pack mule, anyway?" he said.

"We all have our talents," said Todtman.

Ren giggled nervously. They all grabbed flashlights. They were smaller this time, but very powerful. They cut through the murk like wannabe lightsabers.

"Train coming," said Todtman. "Switch off the lights and step in here. Quickly, please!"

Todtman and Ren jumped into narrow gaps along the wall as the train approached. Alex paused to take a last look back as the tunnel began to fill with light. *This is so cool*, he thought. He finally cut back to join the others. But the track was an obstacle course of rails and ties and changing levels.

His foot caught the edge of the deeper channel in the centre of the track, and with a sharp jab of pain he turned his left ankle. His leg bent forward and his knee smacked the metal rail.

"OW!" he said.

"Get up!" shouted Ren. "Get off the tracks!"

The track had begun to glow with reflected light. The ground under him was rumbling hard now. He pushed himself to his feet.

The train's big air horn sounded: *HOOOOOONNNNKKK!*

Had the driver seen him? Could he stop the train in time? Alex took two quick hopping steps and reached the wall. He saw two indentations – and two people filling them.

Todtman shouted something but the thunder of the train drowned it out.

He pointed: left.

Alex saw it now: a third shallow gap against the wall, a pit of shadow in the growing light. He lunged forward and his left leg buckled, but he regained his balance. Two more quick hobbled steps and he was there. He threw himself against the grimy wall.

His back was to the tracks, but it was too late to turn around. With his face plastered to the wall, he couldn't tell if any part of him was sticking out. Alex sucked in his stomach.

The train hit like a tidal wave of noise and force. Alex's teeth chattered and his hair was whipped around by the wind. The gap between each car sang out like a passing bullet, and for one horrifying second, Alex thought the force of the rushing air would suck him out of the pocket. Finally, the last car passed. Alex exhaled and patted himself down to make sure all his parts were still there.

Ren glared over at him, her train-whipped hair giving her a mad scientist look. This time he knew he had it coming. He looked down at the tricky, uneven ground, his pulse pounding in his ears.

"You idiot!" Ren yelled.

"This way, children," called Todtman.

Ren walked after him, and Alex followed, limping slightly. As they continued down the tunnel, Alex's ankle and knee began to feel better. His limp faded, his eyes adjusted, and his skull stopped vibrating. An old tunnel split off from the main one and headed deeper into darkness. "Is this it?" said Alex.

Ren glanced at him without answering and then looked away. He could see she was still mad at him, still giving him the cold shoulder.

"I think so," said Todtman. He turned to look back the way they'd come. They could hear the noise of another train starting to build and see the tunnel starting to brighten. Alex didn't want to go through that again, and Ren was thinking the same thing.

"Let's go," she called, stepping into the new tunnel.

Alex and Todtman followed. They were five feet in by the time the train passed, and Alex pressed his hands over his ears to block out its roar. The beams of their flashlights zigzagged and danced over the dried-out debris and rubble on the abandoned tracks. The new tunnel smelled like a basement. For a while, the only sound was their careful footsteps and their breathing as they sucked in the hot, damp air.

"Doctor?" said Alex, his skin prickling with nerves.

"Yes?"

"That guard at the bridge. . ."

"Poor man."

"It wasn't a heart attack, was it?"

"I don't think so. More like. . ."

"A soul attack?" Alex offered. "What he was going to do to us?"

No one answered, but they all swung their flashlights around the dark tunnel. Alex's bravado had faded along with the light, and the near miss with the train had rattled him. Now, in this dark, abandoned tunnel, he thought he was just about as scared as he could get. But then. . .

"Did you hear something?" he said.

"No," Ren said warily. "Wait . . . I think I heard it this time. Like a scratch-scratch kind of thing?"

"Yeah," said Alex. "I don't like it."

They swung their flashlights around, but the narrow beams revealed nothing. The darkness took away Alex's sight but made him more aware of his other senses. A drop of sweat trailed down his cheek and he tracked its movement with his skin, feeling each nerve cell fire. His chest rose and fell, his breathing faster now.

Another muffled scratch. His ears told him which direction: in front of him and a little to the left. He continued forward, and a little to the right, washing the floor with his flashlight. A few steps later, he felt something on his sneaker and kicked out reflexively. Something smacked against the tunnel wall – *klack!*

He aimed his flashlight at the spot and saw a

shadow slipping out of the light. His pulse pounded. The sound was all around them now, like an animal working its way through dry leaves.

Todtman switched off his flashlight, and the tunnel got even darker.

"What are you doing?" called Ren. "Turn it back on!"

Instead, Todtman reached up and closed his hand around his amulet. Light began pouring out of the gaps between his fingers, weak at first and then very strong. Alex looked directly at it and was momentarily dazzled. His vision cleared.

Scorpions.

Everywhere.

Alex swallowed hard. The air had a venomous tang to it. The scorpions were on the floor, on the concrete pilings, on top of the old steel rails. Their exoskeletons clicked against the tracks and pushed against the dry trash along the ground. Their stingers bobbed above them on the tips of their curled tails.

Alex looked down. There was a small, pale scorpion a foot in front of him. He kicked at it with his sneaker and knocked it on to its back. It righted itself and resumed its march. There was another one behind it, harder to see because it was as black as the ground. No wait, there were two of those. He took a step backwards and felt a crunch. He didn't need to look down to know what he'd stepped on.

"Uh, Doctor?" squeaked Ren. She seemed to be the only one who could speak at the moment. Alex turned to her and saw a scorpion crest her shoulder like a triumphant mountain climber. Before he could even point, she felt the tickle and brushed it away – oblivious – like it was a loose strand of hair.

"Ren, that was—" Alex began, but he was cut short.

"RUN!" shouted Todtman.

They barrelled down the tracks. Alex saw a foot-high pile of old paper in front of him. He nearly ploughed right through it, but at the last second he saw that it was crawling with small, pale scorpions. He leapt over it. He felt his foot slip as it pulped a scorpion. He regained his balance and kept running. His chest tightened with both effort and fear. His lungs burned.

The beam of his flashlight bounced crazily in front of him as he ran. Todtman was behind him, and that meant the light from the amulet was, too.

Where's Ren? He looked back and saw her sticking close to Todtman. He swung his head back around just in time to avoid slamming into a metal post.

"Look for a platform!" Todtman called out. "We need to get off the tracks. They are worse climbers than you think."

Alex looked around. It was true. They had eight legs like spiders, but he didn't see any on the walls. He seriously hoped they weren't on the ceiling, either. Up ahead, he saw it: the edge of the old Worth Street station. He sucked in a ragged breath and called, "Over here!"

He reached the edge of the platform and found himself eye-to-claw with a scorpion so large it looked like a baby lobster. He looked the massive arachnid in the eyes: all twelve of them. Panting deeply, his face coated with sweat, he closed his hand around the amulet. *The wind that comes before the rain.* The scorpion went flying end over end and out of sight. He tossed his flashlight on to the platform and hoisted himself up.

Footsteps slapped behind him, and he turned and pulled Ren up off the tracks. "Are you OK?" he huffed.

"Seriously creeped out," she puffed, a thick drop

of sweat hanging from the tip of her nose. "But yeah, I think so." The drop fell.

They leaned forward to help Todtman up. He let go of his amulet and the light coming from it faded. That's when they realized that they didn't need it any more. The old station was already lit.

They checked the platform and walls for scorpions, then collapsed against it. Alex could see the details of the old subway station, like a tile mosaic that spelled out *Worth St*, but swoops of spray paint covered everything else. They were at the end of the platform, and towards the middle there was a curtain up, cutting off their view.

As their breathing calmed and their pulses stopped pounding in their ears, they became aware of other sounds. They heard muffled clangs and thumps and the not-so-distant sound of human voices.

Electric lights, like the kind found at construction sites, illuminated Alex and Ren as they stood up. Only Todtman looked down. Slowly, he pulled his left pant leg up, just above the top of his sock.

Alex nudged Ren and pointed. They all saw it now. The wound was high on his ankle and already beginning to swell. Todtman looked up and forced a weak grin on to his face. "Stung, I'm afraid."

He winced as he let the pant leg drop, and again as he stood up.

"How bad is it?" asked Alex.

Todtman took a few steps, limping badly. "I'll find out soon," he said. "I didn't see what kind it was. It's the smaller ones that are most dangerous."

"The pale ones?" said Ren.

"Yes."

"How will we know if it was one of them?" said Alex.

"Because there's a good chance I will die." He forced another smile, but this one fooled no one.

"And if it was one of the big ones?"

"Then I will merely be in incredible pain. Now, let's go see what all that noise is about."

Alex took a deep breath. The part of him that wanted to find his mother hoped that the Stung Man was somewhere up ahead. The part of him that wanted to stay safe hoped he wasn't. There was no question which part of him was stronger. He strode forward and took the lead.

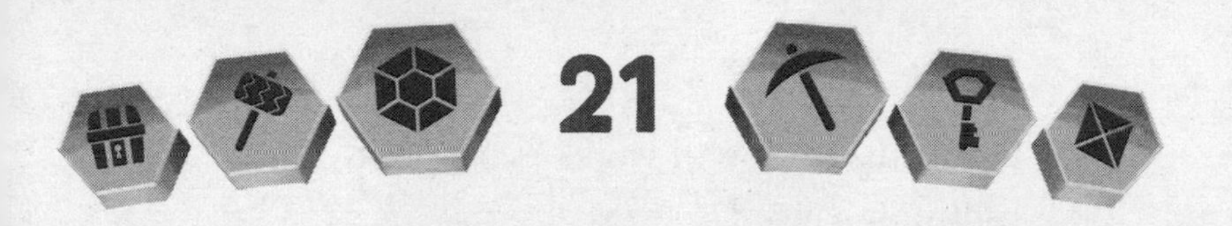

21

INTO THE TOMB

The centre of the platform was hidden behind a grey curtain hanging down from the ceiling and wrapping around in a semicircle. It reminded Alex of the *Under Construction* curtains at the Met, but this one was much larger and made of a heavy material that muffled the strange sounds coming from behind it. He and Ren approached it slowly so Todtman could keep up. He was grimacing from the pain but still focused. "If we find the Stung Man," he said to Alex, "you know what you must do."

"Are you sure it will work?" said Alex.

Todtman paused.

"No."

"Wow," said Ren. "Might've been better if you lied to us on that one."

Todtman shrugged. "I think it will work. . ." He looked at Ren, started over. "I *believe* it will – if Alex made the right choice."

Alex looked at both of them. "No pressure or anything," he said.

Ren glanced at him. "No offence, but do you think I should have made the choice?"

Alex didn't even pretend to be offended. He wished she could.

"Wearing the scarab comes with responsibilities, including the choice," said Todtman. "Besides, how much do you know about ancient funereal texts?"

"Good point," said Ren.

Alex looked away. *How much did* he *know about them?*

As they reached the curtain, the sounds of construction became louder. They found a long flap running just off centre. "Ready?" said Todtman, one hand on the flap, the other on his amulet.

Alex clasped his own amulet and Ren doubled

her grip on her flashlight, holding it like a club. "Ready," they said.

Todtman pulled back the curtain. As soon as it was open, the noise became ten times louder. A power saw whined as its diamond-edged blade cut through stone. Steel chains rattled as they slid through a large pulley. Todtman paused for a second and then stepped inside as sneakily as he could. Alex and Ren took deep breaths and followed.

Half a dozen of the beefiest construction workers Alex had ever seen cut and chipped and chiselled away at a large stone structure. None of them even looked up. They continued to work, their eyes blank and their shirts drenched with sweat.

The massive lion statue reclined in front of a tall opening in the back wall. *No chiselling necessary*, Alex knew. Lions were a symbol of power in ancient Egypt, guardians of the eastern and western horizon. Meanwhile, Ren stared at the facade the men were constructing. Lengths of marble column had been cut into sections and lined up in front of it.

It didn't take long to find the missing stone blocks from the bridge, either. Alex was so fixated on the individual pieces that it took him a few moments to realize what they were looking at. "It's a tomb," he said.

It reminded him of the large tomb in the first room of the Egyptian wing at the Met, a big stone structure that provided a bold introduction to a culture where people often spent more on their tombs than their homes. But as impressive as it looked, this was just the front. The halved columns and chunky capstones framed a twelve-foot-tall passage leading deeper into the abandoned station. The lion stood guard out front.

"They're re-creating it for him," said Todtman, edging forward. His voice betrayed a certain grudging admiration for the work. "It's the Stung Man's tomb."

"And it will be yours, as well," a voice called out.

Al-Dab'u stepped out from the shadowy mouth of the tomb and advanced directly towards them. He wore the mask, and his guard's uniform had been replaced by a ratty brown robe that Alex could smell from ten feet away.

All his instincts shouted: *Danger! Run!*

But he held his ground. They'd come here, tracked the creature to its den, and they were staying.

They were fighting.

But they weren't the only ones.

All around them, the workers turned from their tasks and began moving towards them, power tools in hand. "Uh-oh. . ." Alex heard himself say. Al-Dab'u's hand shot up from his side in one fast motion, and Alex saw Todtman twist and then stiffen. Al-Dab'u squeezed his hand closed as he raised it up. Six feet away, a small gasp escaped from Todtman's mouth as his feet slowly left the ground.

"He's crushing him!" shouted Ren. She yanked at him, trying to pull him back down to the ground.

Al-Dab'u ignored her and concentrated on Todtman's reddening face. Alex reached for the scarab, but he had no idea what to do. Wind would just ruffle Al-Dab'u's robe, and this man clearly didn't fear marbles. *Maybe if I bull-rush him, break his concentration. . .* That's when he saw the first mammoth construction worker approaching with his shovel raised in the air.

Ren saw it, too. She lifted her flashlight like a club: a very small Viking preparing to charge. But Alex reached over and grabbed her shoulder: *Wait.*

He took one more look at Todtman: frozen a foot off the floor and slowly being suffocated.

Alex smiled.

"Are you crazy?" shouted Ren. "He's *crushing* him!"

Alex just nodded towards Todtman's hand. Al-Dab'u had clamped down a second too late. Todtman's hand already held his falcon amulet. The worker slammed the shovel into Al-Dab'u's shoulder, sending him reeling.

Todtman dropped to the ground, bending his bad leg slightly to land on his good one. He took a quick breath. "Go!" he wheezed. "To the tomb!"

Al-Dab'u climbed to his feet as Alex and Ren sprinted around him towards the tomb. They headed for the passage Al-Dab'u had just exited, which cut directly into the stone and concrete of the old subway station. They darted between the heavy grey columns and into the eerie tunnel.

Alex stopped to get his bearings and realized that Todtman wasn't with them. He risked a quick look back and saw the German was still on the platform, crouched defensively, while Al-Dab'u warily circled him, holding his shoulder. It seemed they had both learned something from their previous encounter. Alex felt like he was witnessing the end of a knife fight. And not necessarily a fair one: thug versus professor, death cult versus book club.

Ren turned to look. "We can't just leave him there," she said.

Alex knew she had a point. Al-Dab'u's mask seemed to be at least as powerful as Todtman's amulet, and it wasn't clear whose side the other workers would take. Todtman seemed to sense their hesitation and glanced at them over his shoulder. "Go!" he shouted again.

Alex turned to Ren: "We have to find the Stung Man! But we'll come back."

Ren's face was a mask of fear and indecision, but with one last look back, she followed Alex deeper into the tomb. She hoped there'd be someone left to come back to. The passage was surprisingly deep, extending well past the original station. There were hieroglyphic symbols along the walls and a faint glow that seemed to come from the ceiling itself.

Ren stumbled as she stared up at the light, and Alex pulled a few feet ahead. His hand was around his amulet. "I can read these now," he said, his eyes full of wonder. "Most of them. I think it's the scarab!"

Ren nodded, adding it to the list of things she wasn't allowing herself to really process just yet. She had no idea how the amulets worked, but she definitely wanted one. *Like the world's best iPhone*, she thought. Instead, she was left fighting the undead with a flashlight and a vague memory of first-grade tae kwon do.

They followed the passage deep into the surrounding stone until they reached an intersection.

"Which way?" she said.

"Do you even have to ask?" said Alex, pointing at the floor of the passage on the left.

"Right," she said. "Of course. It's the one with the scorpions."

She remembered what Todtman had said: *The small ones are more venomous.* Fortunately, they were also easier to kick aside and stomp on. She just hoped their needlelike stingers couldn't get through the soles of her shoes.

She was side by side with Alex now, a united front of stomping sneakers and wide-open eyes, moving as fast as they dared. Ten feet into the new passage, they heard a grinding sound coming from the floor. She saw Alex's head shoot to the left and the right, reading the hieroglyphs on the walls.

"Jump!" he said.

They took a running jump forward as the floor snapped open beneath them. Alex cleared it with six inches to spare. But he was taller. Ren got the tip of her front sneaker on the edge – and that was it.

"Alex!" she called. Her back leg swung behind her over the open pit, her arms windmilling wildly to try to keep her weight forward. Ten feet below, the bottom was a living carpet of scorpions.

Alex reached back for her, but her flailing arm knocked his hand away. She began to tip back. . .

His arms wrapped tightly around her and yanked her forward on to the path. They tumbled over, her head swimming with relief.

"Got you!" Alex crowed.

Ren's nerves were a jumbled mess, but she pushed Alex away, got to her feet, and tried to get it together. "Oh, great," she managed. "Traps."

They kept moving down the hallway, more cautiously now. Alex had put a few more feet between them when she heard him yell again, "Duck!"

Duck? A thick, slick sound filled the passage and Ren instinctively froze. There was a thin layer of sweat on her face, neck and arms now, and she felt a light wind brush against it, chilling her.

She saw a flash of movement and her eyes widened in horror. A four-foot steel blade was swinging directly towards her. At a dead stop, with no time to react, all she could do was close her eyes and scream.

"NO!" shouted Alex from just up ahead.

Ren was braced for the slash of the blade, but all she felt was a breeze ruffle her hair.

And then she felt nothing.

She opened her eyes – which were somehow still attached to her body. "What happened?" she gasped.

Alex stood stock-still in front of her, his face frozen but his eyes practically spinning.

"Alex?" Ren asked.

"It . . . it went right over you!" he gasped. "I guess they weren't expecting such a short grave robber!"

Ren met Alex's eyes and suddenly they were both laughing hysterically.

First time being short ever did me any good, thought Ren.

A few steps later, Ren's wash of relief turned to cold fear in a whiplash reversal. She didn't even know what the sound was at first – just two sharp mechanical *snick*s – but she knew it wasn't good.

Two narrow posts popped up along the walls, with vicious-looking wire strung between them in an X pattern, like a shoelace. There would be no jumping or ducking this trap. The wicked wires gleamed in the light and then there was another *snick* from deep inside the wall and the posts shot forward. *It's going to slice us into chunks!* thought Ren.

There was no time to turn and run – and a blade and pit were waiting, anyway. All Ren could do was raise her flashlight up in front of her. Alex clutched his amulet with one hand and snapped his fingers with the other. It seemed like an odd final gesture.

This time Ren's eyes seemed glued open as the deadly steel approached her skin. If she was going to go down, she'd go down swinging. She lashed out with her flashlight and hit a strand of wire. The thin steel cut a groove into the heavy plastic handle, but the wire was already unravelling, pulling apart as it whipped past. She felt a sting on her arm and another on her neck and then nothing.

Ren lightly touched the wound on her neck. It didn't feel like much more than a paper cut. Then again, those hurt.

"Are you OK?" she called to Alex.

He turned back, a long, thin line of blood forming on his forehead. "I think so," he said.

"What did you do?" she said.

"I snapped it," he said, waving his amulet. "Top corner, like a shoelace. . . I'm pretty good at breaking stuff with this thing!"

Yep, thought Ren. *I want one of those.*

The end of the tunnel was just up ahead now. They stepped through – and into the inner sanctum of the Stung Man.

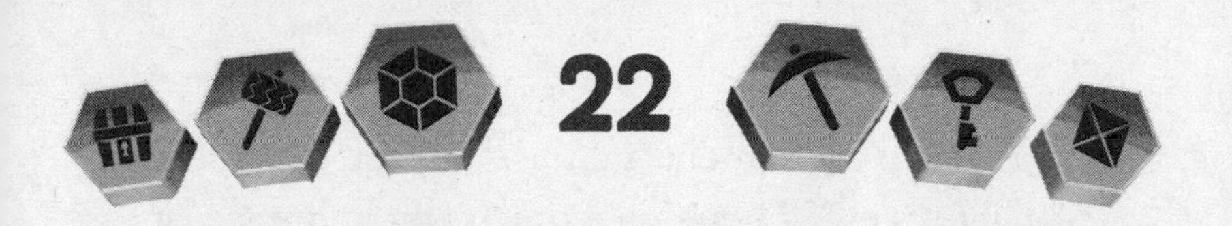

22

THE FINAL SHOWDOWN

The first things Alex noticed about the chamber were the fancy tapestries that hung from the walls and the luxurious rugs on the stone floors. Then he realized that a three-foot-high stone pool in the centre of the room was providing the light, a ghostly glow rising from the water inside.

His head swam as he looked at the luminous liquid. Somewhere above was the city and the sunlight he knew, but it seemed painfully distant. He felt confined and constricted by this place. By this *tomb.*

A slight movement in the back of the room caught his eye. There, on a rough-hewn throne, sat the Stung Man.

"There he is," whispered Ren, her lips barely giving shape to the air leaving her lungs.

Alex tried to answer but failed.

Unlike the mummy clad in ragged scraps at the museum, this man was now clothed in regal robes. The angry welts and stings were still there, but the rest of his skin looked almost normal now. He rose to meet them. "I wasn't expecting visitors," he said, but only Alex understood.

"Is he speaking, like, Egyptian?" whispered Ren.

Ancient Egyptian, realized Alex, still clutching his amulet in a death grip.

It was terrifying, of course, to hear a dead man speak. The first ice-water shock of fear hit Alex and his knees flexed, but he didn't run. He'd come all this way, and one word kept him there.

Mom.

What if she was nearby? What if she was in a chamber somewhere in this terrible tomb?

She'd done everything for him. He wouldn't abandon her.

But now what?

I'm in a room with a walking corpse. There's no denying it. He's right in front of me. Now what?

He scanned the room, getting his bearings, readying for a fight. In between two tapestries, he saw a vertical gash in the stone. There were raised white columns on either side, and the gap between them was painted a reddish orange: a false door.

The Stung Man stepped down into the room. His movements showed none of the stiffness from before. He moved fluidly, Alex noted uneasily, like the master thief he had once been. "Do you like it?" the Stung Man asked, gesturing around the room.

"What is he *saying*?" said Ren, her voice a mix of desperation and anger.

The Stung Man frowned, realizing he had only half the audience.

He turned to Alex.

"But you understand me, don't you?"

Alex managed a weak nod. He understood him perfectly, not just his words but also his intent. With every word, and every step, the Stung Man edged closer. He had reached the large, glowing pool, and he tapped his fingers lightly on the edge as he began to walk around it.

"I know about you," said Alex, his voice finally returning.

"Oh yes? And what is it you know?"

He can understand me, too. Alex continued. "I know how you. . . I know what happened to you."

"Do you?"

Alex nodded nervously. The Stung Man was halfway around the pool. With every step the robed figure took, the amulet grew warmer in Alex's hand, and the pulse grew stronger in his head.

"Perhaps you know the story," said the Stung Man. "But do you really imagine you know what it was like, crouched there in that hot, dark cave?"

Alex's imagination failed him. How could he concentrate with a predator approaching? *This man is going to* consume *us.*

He could feel Ren practically vibrating with fear.

"The stings I could feel but not see?" the Stung Man continued. "The wounds in my skin and the venom spreading like burning oil under it? You think you *know*? The stings that would not stop, even after I'd fallen: on my face, my neck, the soles of my feet?"

"Do you understand him?" whispered Ren, tugging at Alex's arm. "*What* is he *saying*?"

Alex knew how terrified she must be, but he didn't have time to stop and translate. He had to try something, had to stall him.

"I know why you did it, too," he called.

The Stung Man tilted his head. "Oh yes?"

"I know that if it wasn't for the pharaoh, you would've been planting crops not stealing jewels. I know you mostly stole from him."

A familiar rattling noise started up. The four canopic jars were nestled in the corners of the room.

"And you think that makes me a hero?"

"I don't think it makes you a villain."

The Stung Man let out a quick, sharp breath, amused. He was around the pool now. "You misunderstand me, little boy."

"I read it. . ." Alex began, but the towering figure paid him no mind.

"This world took everything from me!" the Stung Man shouted. Alex jumped at the sudden volume. "Everything! And now, I intend to take it back!"

Alex heard four loud pops and turned in time to see the alabaster lid hop off the nearest canopic jar. As it fell to the floor, a stream of scorpions – ten, twenty, a hundred – began pouring from the jar's open neck. Around the room, the same thing was happening with the other jars. The rattling was quickly replaced by the clicking and clacking of scorpions.

Alex's mouth fell open in horror as Ren's opened to scream.

"Don't worry about my little friends," said the Stung Man.

The scorpions spread out in a thick, writhing line along the sides of the room. They spilled out into the passageway but didn't advance inward. They climbed over each other, claws out, stingers poised: a living border to prevent any attempt at escape.

"You see?" said the Stung Man. "They're just here to do a job. I'm the one you have to worry about."

He was closer now, too close.

"Use the Book of the Dead!" called Ren.

But Alex had another plan. He tried the move he'd used before with the amulet. Squeezing the scarab with his left hand, he pushed his right hand forward. A phantom wind rose up and the tapestries against the far wall flapped wildly as the water in the pool formed waves that slopped over the sides. But the Stung Man kept coming. His movement was slowed a little but not nearly enough. He smiled.

"I am awake now, child." He pulled his left hand

back inside the heavy crimson sleeve of his robe. "And I have all kinds of tricks up my sleeve."

When his hand slid back out, it had transformed into a massive scorpion stinger. The barb was as long and sharp as a carving knife. A large drop of amber venom glistened on the tip.

"Oh, you have got to be *kidding me*!" Ren shouted.

Unable to step backwards because of the skittering line of scorpions, she took a few hops to the side.

Alex's stomach twisted with fear. He scanned the room for some small projectile to launch and redoubled the wind, but the Stung Man continued to advance.

"Alex, the Book!" Ren shouted again. She yanked the backpack off of him.

"OK, OK!" said Alex. His voice shook. He hadn't forgotten the plan. He just didn't think it was a very good one. He'd counted on the amulet, but it wasn't enough. Alex had led them – led Ren! – to their deaths, and there was very little he could do about it. Twin jets of fear and adrenaline coursed through him. There was only one thing left to try. He pulled out a round plastic container that held the scrolls.

The Stung Man stopped in his tracks. "You have the Prayers?"

"That's right, tomb breath!" called Alex, trying to sound brave.

The Stung Man gave Alex a wolfish grin. "I see I am not the only thief here."

Alex ignored the jab. With the exhibition closed, Todtman was in charge of the Book's safekeeping. They were just borrowing the scrolls.

The question, the Big Question: Had they borrowed the right one?

There were over two hundred spells, many dealing with obscure aspects of the afterlife. The spell for "Not Being Scalded by Hot Water in the Afterlife" wasn't going to do them much good. And it seemed a little late for the famous "Declaration of the Soul's Innocence", too. Todtman believed that the right spell would send the Stung Man back. Alex had brought three, and he now realized just how ridiculous that was. They didn't have time for three spells! What was the Stung Man going to do, watch a movie while he tried them all?

He would get one chance. One. His fingers trembling, he reached for the ancient scrolls.

"Oh, but it's just a few of them," said the Stung

Man, clearly disappointed. He circled towards the friends and they circled away. He was clearly enjoying toying with them.

"Yeah, guess which one," said Alex, pulling the first roll free from the canister, his unsteady fingers nearly tearing what looked to be very old papyrus. He willed his mind to slow down and consider his choices. His first choice: "To help the soul rejoin the body in the afterlife."

No, he thought.

The Stung Man took a step closer.

He threw the scroll down. This soul had already rejoined its corpse – and not in the afterlife. He tugged the second scroll free.

No time to hesitate, no margin for error.

He filled his lungs, preparing for the chant.

"I'd love to hear your choice," said the Stung Man. "I'm quite sure it's wrong. But I can't take that chance. I just got back, you see."

And with that, he flicked his hand. The scroll yanked free from Alex's grasp and flew across the room. The first syllable of the chant – a long, resonant "Hemmm" – died on his lips.

The scroll hit the wall and fell into the corner, landing on the backs of a few dozen angry scorpions. "I'll get it!" called Ren, not sounding at all convinced.

Alex was amazed: *She's acting.* At a time like this: full of fear, in over her head, unarmed, understanding nothing that was being said, she was doing her part.

"There's another spell, you know," the Stung Man said to him. "It is for 'Washing the Mouth of Foolish Words'. Perhaps I'll recite it for you. Of course, I'll kill you first – it *is* for the dead."

The Stung Man struck out with his left hand. The stinger flew towards Alex on the end of a long, segmented tail. Alex ducked, bad dodgeball memories filling his mind. The stinger shot over his shoulder and slammed into the wall behind him.

Alex turned in time to see the stinger draw back towards him. He squawked and ducked again, touching a hand down for balance and missing a scorpion by inches.

"Impressive reflexes," said the Stung Man. "But it doesn't matter." He reached out with his right hand and slowly raised it. Across the room, what felt like invisible metal bands tightened around Alex's body, locking him in place. It was the same thing Al-Dab'u had done to Todtman. But Todtman had spent years preparing for this sort of thing. Alex had spent days. All he could do was watch as his body was slowly lifted off the floor. His feet dangled in the air, his heart raced, his lungs pressed inward, and he struggled for breath. He felt his mind flicker on the edge of collapse.

The ancient menace walked slowly towards him. His right hand was stretched out in front of him, holding Alex in the air. His stinger was cocked back, ready for the death blow.

The bands around him tightened and Alex's vision began to narrow. He viewed his last seconds as if through a tunnel.

"Got it!" yelled Ren, standing on tiptoes and shaking the last few scorpions off the scroll.

The Stung Man's head whipped around.

"How do you read this, anyway?" said Ren, squinting at the odd symbols. "This one looks like a snake."

"Give that to me, little girl!" said the Stung Man. He dropped his right hand and Alex fell to the ground with a thump.

"Oh, wait, I remember now," said Ren. "Doctor Todtman said something about. . ."

Alex recognized her bluff, but the Stung

Man didn't know her so well. He took a few long steps towards her and pointed the stinger at her stomach. "Give the scroll to me and I promise to kill you quickly." It was probably lucky Ren couldn't understand his words.

"Hemmm!" she chanted, imitating Alex.

Her imitation was so good that it took the Stung Man a moment to realize that Alex was chanting again, too. It wasn't until the second word – "Nesoot" – that he spun back around.

Ren echoed him: "Nesoot!" The Stung Man turned again. Alex and Ren both had scrolls now.

The Stung Man gave a great bellow of rage.

Alex's voice cracked, but he couldn't stop chanting.

"For the Tilling of the Rich Soil of the Afterlife. . ."

A farmer's prayer.

Even in the afterlife – especially in the afterlife – the Stung Man couldn't escape who he really was.

The Stung Man growled like an animal. "Say no more!" he commanded, but his voice, so oily before, grew thicker with each word.

The stinger shot out again, flying through the air towards Ren. Her eyes wide with fear, she scanned the floor for a safe spot to step as time ran out.

The barb struck not her but the scroll, punching a hole straight through and leaving Ren frozen with shock. The Stung Man pulled the stinger back towards him, but the yellow paper ripped in half as he did. He didn't know exactly what paper was – the modern form hadn't been invented when he was entombed. Nor, for that matter, had museum gift shops that sold reproduction scrolls. But he knew something wasn't right. He knew that wasn't brittle papyrus his stinger had just torn through.

He turned to face Alex, who continued to steadily chant each word and symbol from the real scroll that had been hidden in his backpack the whole time.

"Treachery!" called the Stung Man. He rushed towards Alex, but his muscles aged and tightened with each step. He kept going, driven by the indomitable will that had allowed him to cling to the edge of the afterlife for millennia. He pointed the stinger at Alex. The point was still sharp, but the bulb had dried and hollowed.

As Alex chanted, the writing seemed to come alive on the page. The lines glowed and the symbols danced, and he watched transfixed as his mouth gave voice to the glittering text. The Stung Man was five feet away, four feet. The skin pulled tight on his skull, threatening to split. Three feet away. The hand that reached out for the scroll was shrivelled and leathery.

The Stung Man was two feet away when Alex finished the chant. The dried corpse toppled and fell. Alex stepped back and let it, the glowing text fading in his hands.

All around them, the scorpions were sucked back into their jars like so much click-clacking smoke. The alabaster lids were pulled on last, closing tight. The light from the pool began to fade. Out in the passageway, the light began to fade as well.

Ren rushed over. "Are you OK?"

Alex nodded. He was getting a major headache, but it didn't seem worth mentioning. They both stared down at the Stung Man, laid out before them, a mummy once more.

"We're alive," said Alex.

Standing in the growing dark, Ren paused to consider the sheer improbability of the statement.

"For the moment," she said, clicking on her flashlight. The remains of a smashed scorpion were smeared on the lens, casting on odd sort of bat signal on the ceiling of the chamber.

"The doctor. . ." she said.

Alex nodded. The last time they'd seen Todtman, he was wounded and outnumbered.

The two friends headed back down the passageway as fast as they dared, their eyes still wide, their pulses still racing. They knew there was danger in the darkness.

23

A NEW PATH

They made it back through the passage intact. The traps were the same on the way out, and Ren hadn't grown any taller. The leap over the pit was a little scary in the dark, but now she knew what to expect. Once they landed on the other side, their worries immediately shifted back to Todtman.

Their worries were misplaced.

They emerged from the tomb to find someone hopelessly outnumbered, but it wasn't Todtman. The scorpion sting had dropped him to the floor –

he was kneeling, right knee up and left knee down – but everything else was going quite well.

One of the construction workers was closing in on Al-Dab'u from the left with a raised hammer. Another approached from the right with a power drill.

Todtman watched them like a proud papa. The other workers formed a circle around the action: reinforcements. From a distance, Alex thought it had the look of a school-yard fight. Well, except for the power tools.

"They switched sides," said Ren. "All of them."

"He's controlling them," said Alex. He understood now. "Remember what he said, 'A watcher can also be a boss, an overseer'?"

"That's pretty boss," agreed Ren.

Al-Dab'u extended his hand menacingly as the workers closed in, first twisting one to the floor, then crushing the breath from another, but he was surrounded and couldn't take them all at once. His mask pivoted around, its permanent grin now looking comically optimistic. The hollow eyes swept over Alex and Ren. He didn't know how they had returned from the tomb alive, but he knew what it meant.

He swung back, his ratty robe briefly whirling into a bell shape. With one final wave of his hand, the worker closest to him was sent reeling. Todtman sent what looked like the fastest of the construction crew after him, but Al-Dab'u was too quick. He leapt through the heavy curtain. Alex wondered if he remembered that the edge of the old subway platform was right on the other side. A loud thump told him he had not.

Alex and Ren ran over to Todtman. "Are you OK?" asked Ren.

"I've been better," said Todtman.

Alex was surprised to see that, despite the pain he must be feeling, Todtman was wearing a weary smile. "Well," he said, looking down modestly. "It *is* more exciting than cataloguing pottery." He let his hand fall from his amulet.

He tried to stand, but his left leg wouldn't hold him. Alex and Ren got on either side of him and pulled him up. A fog seemed to lift from the construction workers, and they milled around the platform in confusion.

"Manny, is that you?" said one.

"Yeah, it's me, Rich," said Manny. "But where *are* we?"

"Hey," said Rich. "Look at that. It's the library lion!"

The workers all turned to look, seeing it for the first time with wide, startled eyes.

"The library is going to want that back," said Ren.

"I think we will be able to arrange that," said Todtman. "Eventually, anyway. For now, it may be a little . . . overdue."

Ren shook her head. "Imagine the fine. . ."

"Hey, who are you guys?" said Manny, zeroing in on the trio. "What are you doing here? What are *we* doing here?"

"I hate to do this," said Todtman, reaching up and grasping his amulet.

"Do what?" said Manny. A moment later, his eyes went blank again.

Alex and Ren looked around. All the workers had the placid expressions and drooping posture of sleepwalkers. Todtman whispered a few words in what Alex now recognized as an ancient Egyptian dialect. One by one, the construction workers wandered towards the flap of the heavy grey curtain.

"They will return to the surface with a few days missing and vague memories of a trip to Philadelphia," said Todtman. "I hope it doesn't cause them too much trouble."

Alex watched the last one slip through the curtain, relieved not to hear any loud thumps on the other side this time. Something occurred to him.

"Is that what you did to the detective?" said Alex. "He's been kind of sleepwalking through the investigation, too."

"I may have had a little talk with him," admitted Todtman. He looked over at Alex and now he noticed something: "You're hurt."

Alex reached up and touched the long, thin cut left by the razor wire. A few flecks of dried blood flaked off on his fingertips. "Trust me," he said, "my head feels a lot worse on the inside."

Todtman turned to Ren: "You're cut, too."

"Nothing major," she said, looking down at the cut on her arm.

"The scroll worked, then?" said Todtman. "Was it the first one?"

"The second," said Alex, but there was no triumph in his voice. Something was still troubling him.

"Yes, a farmer, after all," said Todtman, attempting a step and nearly falling.

"You need to get to a hospital," said Ren.

"I know a good one," said Alex. "But we can't . . . I mean. . ." He forced himself to take a breath. All the adrenaline, the rush of all that fear, it all poured out of him in two quick words. "My mom!"

"You saw no sign of her?" asked Todtman.

"No," said Alex. "But there was another direction, another tunnel."

Ren nodded emphatically.

"We must have a look, then," said Todtman.

Alex wanted to run back inside. Instead, he had to walk – and slowly. He propped himself under Todtman's right arm as Ren supported his left, and they headed through the open mouth of the tomb. Todtman reached up to his amulet and turned the "lights" back on.

"You're good with lights," said Ren.

"A watcher needs to see."

Alex and Ren warned him about the traps they'd encountered in the left passage. They moved slowly as they entered the passage on their right, and Todtman focused his senses with his amulet. But they encountered nothing.

"It feels too easy," said Todtman, but Alex and Ren weren't going to complain about that.

As they neared the end of the tunnel, they saw dim light coming from an open doorway.

"I don't like it," said Todtman, his eyes scanning the floor and ceiling ahead. "Let's stop here for a second."

"Good idea," said Ren. "This place is trap central."

Alex couldn't believe this. The traps were the other way, just like the scorpions had been. This was the last room left. His mom *had to be* in there.

They can wait if they want to, he thought, *I've waited enough.*

"She's in there," said Alex. "She has to be!"

And then another thought hit him, the one that was never far away: *What if she's suffering?*

He wriggled out from under Todtman's arm and took off at a run. "Come on!" he shouted.

"Wait!" called Todtman.

Alex slowed down just enough to look back, his chest tight with impatience: His *mom* could be up ahead! As he paused, long steel spikes shot up from the floor in front of him, so close that one punched a divot into the rubber tip of his right sneaker. His momentum carried his shoulder into the steel a split second after the point shot past, bringing him to a sudden, jarring halt.

A rumble like thunder sounded above them, the heavy, shifting sound of rock on rock. "This way!"

called Todtman, waving his hand back the way they'd come.

"But. . ." said Alex. He strained for a look into the little room in front of him, his view now cut into sections by the tall spikes.

Ren spelled it out for him: "It's a trap, Alex!"

"Oh!" he gasped. He turned and ran as rocks began raining down. But running was not an option for Todtman – or for Ren, who was the only one left to support him. In his hurry, Alex had left them in the lurch. Now, with the roof of the passage caving in all around them, all he could think to do was shove them both from behind. All three stumbled forward, Todtman barking in pain as his injured ankle gave out.

Todtman and Ren fell face-first into a rising cloud of dust, and Alex tripped over them and did the same. Behind them, the passage was a rock pile.

"That was painful," groaned Todtman.

Ren rose to her knees and looked over at Alex. "You almost got us *killed*."

Alex knew she was right. "Sorry," he mumbled, his face hot under a thin scrim of dust. "I thought my mom was in there."

The anger faded from Ren's face and she looked back at the rocks.

"No one was in there," said Todtman, wincing as he rose to his feet. "It was meant to be *our* tomb."

Alex felt the ground give out underneath him. This time it wasn't a trap. It was despair. "It was a dead end. My mom's not here."

The other two were quiet for a few moments. They'd heard his pain.

"Perhaps," said Todtman, "but let me see this other room."

"We already checked it," said Alex.

"Yeah," agreed Ren. "The only person in there just turned back into leather."

"Just the same," said Todtman. He spread his arms like a falcon about to take flight, and the others took their positions under his arms. Todtman had to limp along the edge above the now-empty scorpion pit. Then Ren tripped the blade intentionally and the three passed by while it was reloading. The split wire merely waved at them.

As they entered the room, Todtman used his amulet to make the central pool glow once more. "This is the tomb chapel," he said as the chamber came into view.

Todtman propped himself against the wall and looked around at the stolen finery. Alex and Ren circled the room from opposite directions. Ren stepped over the Stung Man's well-dressed corpse and "accidentally" kicked it. "Oops," she said.

"See," said Alex, turning back to Todtman. "Empty."

"Yes," he said, "but in ancient Egypt, tomb chapels generally had two rooms: an outer one and. . ."

"An inner one," said Alex. He'd forgotten that part.

They all looked around the chamber. Alex and Todtman clasped their amulets and closed their eyes, hoping for a little extra insight.

"Uh, boys?" said Ren. They opened their eyes and she was at the back of the room, lifting the corner of the largest tapestry. "It's back here."

"How did you know?" said Alex.

"It's the most logical place," she said.

"Like I said before," said Todtman, "we all have our talents."

An unfinished stone box filled the centre of the inner chamber. "A new sarcophagus for a new tomb," said Todtman.

"Why?" said Ren, peering around him.

"What's the phrase," said Todtman, "nap time?"

There was a pair of large copper pots on either

side of the rough-hewn stone. Ren leaned over and sniffed one. “Smells like smoke,” she said.

“Flashlight, please,” said Todtman. Even after they pulled the tapestry down, the pool was far away and the inner room was dim.

Alex pulled one from his backpack.

“Hold it here,” said Todtman, pointing at the pot. Then he began sifting through the piled ashes inside. He pulled out a few scraps of what looked like either paper or cardboard and held them under the flashlight beam. He dropped each one to the floor.

“Nothing,” he said after the last one.

He raised his soot-blackened hand out of the first pot and began sifting through the second.

“What are we looking for?” said Ren.

“These small fires burn unevenly,” said Todtman. “We sometimes recover small artefacts this way.”

He fished around for another minute in silence and then pulled another scrap of paper out. He blew on it and held it under the light. “What does this look like to you?”

Alex leaned in. He saw a black line with a few circles next to it. He took it from Todtman and brushed it off some more. He saw a single smudged name next to one of the circles. "Subway map," he said.

"I guess they didn't know the subways here any better than I did," said Todtman.

"Hey, Ren," said Alex as he dropped the scrap to the floor. "Where's Goodge Street? Is that in Brooklyn?"

"I don't think so," she said. "Sounds kind of Queens-y."

"Did you say 'Goodge Street'?" said Todtman.

"Yeah," said Alex. "What do you think: Brooklyn or Queens?"

"London," said Todtman. "I've been to that station before."

He removed his hands from the pot and brushed them off on his pants: black soot on black cloth. "It's near the British Museum."

Alex's head reeled. It was a clue, a lead... Whatever word he chose, it was *something*. But it wasn't his mom. And this one didn't lead him downtown, or even to Queens. It led across an entire ocean.

He didn't look at Todtman. He didn't want to see his orderly mind processing this latest piece of information.

He didn't look at Ren. He didn't want to see her plugging this new piece into her puzzle.

He looked at the nearest copper pot.

He smacked it on to the floor. Soot and ashes flew.

Once again, the others were quiet. Their minds could process more than just clues.

"Maybe she's in London?" said Ren hopefully.

Alex looked over. He was angry, but not at her.

"It seems The Order is," said Todtman, "or will be."

Alex let out a long, slow breath. He had to be calmer now, smarter.

"And it *is* raining blood over there," he added quietly.

They turned and began their long trek back to daylight, walking slowly. They all had a lot to process now.

Is she slipping away? thought Alex.

Is she already gone?

He had to help her, but he didn't even know where she was.

EPILOGUE

"I nearly lost the leg," said Todtman. "At least that's what they tell me."

Alex and Ren looked at the outline of his left leg under the crisp sheet of his hospital bed. *Still there.* Then they looked back up towards his face, wearing that now familiar froggy smile. He was in good spirits.

"I hate to miss work – German, you know – but I suppose this is a good time for it."

"The whole wing is closed," said Ren.

"Yes, how is Hector?" said Todtman. "Your father's friend, I believe?"

"He looks even worse than you."

"That bad?" said Todtman, frowning.

"Who even gets tuberculosis any more?"

"Very few people," said Todtman. "But it was quite common in ancient Egypt. One of the reasons the Old Kingdom collapsed, actually."

"That's where Hector and the other two were working," said Ren. "In the Old Kingdom rooms."

There was a pause as the information sank in.

"Probably a good thing that wing's closed," said Alex.

"Completely closed," said Ren.

Alex could hear the relief in her voice, and he knew why. The quarantine would keep her dad out of there for now. An image flashed through his mind: the little mummy, tossing and turning unseen in her slumber.

"Yes, I'll have to keep a close eye on it," said Todtman. His amulet stood out against his pyjama top, which was not black but a surprising light blue.

"While we're away. . ." said Alex.

Alex and Ren were headed to London. Officially,

it was their first assignment as Junior Interns to the internationally renowned Dr Ernst Todtman. In reality, strange things were afoot in England, as well.

"What do you think we'll find?" said Ren.

"Some messy sidewalks," volunteered Alex.

Blood had made another appearance in the London rain.

"So gross," said Ren.

"Well, I would definitely bring an umbrella," said Todtman dryly.

"I wish you could come," said Alex.

"I do, too," said Todtman, glancing down at his leg. "But I will have plenty to keep me busy here. Returning a lion and the like. And my colleague will be there. Dr Aditi is a renowned scholar."

"Another member of the book club, you mean?" said Ren.

"Exactly," said Todtman. He turned to Alex and added: "And a good friend of your mother's."

"Do you really think she'll be there?" asked Alex, and they all knew he didn't mean Dr Aditi.

"I hope so," said Todtman. "Something is going on there, and the pattern does seem very familiar."

Alex nodded. In addition to the bloody bad showers, there'd been reports of grave robbery and a near riot at one of the museums. Definitely familiar.

"Do you think one of *them* will be there, too?" said Ren. "Another Death Walker?"

"That is my fear," said Todtman. "You must be careful, and do as Dr Aditi says."

"You sound like my dad," said Ren.

"Yes, he was not so easy to convince," said Todtman.

"You didn't mind-zap him, did you?" Ren asked, staring at him anxiously. "You promised."

Todtman raised his hands. "Innocent," he said. "I just mentioned that these internships are quite common in Germany, that you would be carefully chaperoned, and that it would be a great comfort to Alex."

"I helped with that last part," admitted Alex, raising his hand.

"I may also have mentioned that it looks *very* good on school applications," added Todtman.

Ren could see that last line having an impact. Heck, it had an impact on her: This was Manhattan, where the competition started in pre-K and ended never. Still, she was sceptical. Maybe he'd mind-zapped her mom instead?

"What about my aunt and uncle?" said Alex. "You didn't mind-zap them, did you?"

"I don't remember you asking me not to," said Todtman.

Alex smiled. He hadn't. And he wouldn't miss sleeping under a desk.

Two hours later, they were on their way to the airport. Ren's parents came with them and got a little teary-eyed at the gate. Alex just rode it out.

Ren got the window seat on the plane and gazed out at the runway. She was excited for the trip – London! – but also determined for the mission. She wanted to help Alex and keep him safe. That was a big part of it, but part of it was for her, too. This was her chance to truly be exceptional, and not just look the part. The next time her dad called her his "little Einstein", she wouldn't be embarrassed. Forget Jesse Blatz; could even Einstein do what she was preparing to do? Would he even try?

Alex stared directly at the back of the seat in front of him. He was carrying a heavier weight. He was sure of it now: Everything that was happening was his fault. People had already died because he had lived. All he could do was try to make it right. He had to find the Lost Spells before they could be used again, and he had to undo the damage that had been done.

But more than that, he had to find his mom. She'd taken care of him his whole life, and now it had cost her. Not everything, though. He was sure his mom was still alive. It wasn't some insight imparted by his amulet. It was just a feeling he had. They had always been so close – doting mother and only son. Deep down, he could still feel that connection, stretched thin, but unbroken.

He intended to follow that thread wherever it led. Across an ocean? Sure. Across the globe? If he had to.

For twelve years, he'd been defined by what he couldn't do. He'd spent so much time cautious and fearful, sitting and watching. Now, he'd be defined by what he had to do. And at that moment, as he thought about the dangers that lay ahead in London, he was not afraid.

And not nearly so far away, behind a blue curtain just up the aisle, one final member of the crew reclined in comfort in first class. Luke had been a late addition to the flight. Officially, he was going to London for an elite track-and-field camp. Unofficially, Alex was pretty sure his aunt and uncle were sending Luke to keep an eye on him. Alex wasn't sure if that made his cousin an obstacle or an ally, and Luke wasn't saying either way. A battered Yankees cap pulled down low, he was already asleep.

Thousands of miles away, in the underground lair of The Order, a slumber that had lasted millennia was over. Everything had changed. The heavy sarcophagus at the centre of the chamber sat like an open wound between two worlds. Its stone lid lay cracked in two on the floor. Only the leader dared venture in now. Kneeling, he pointed his golden mask at the floor and listened to the shadowy presence looming above him.

"Rise, loyal servant," came a dry and desolate voice. "For soon, the old ways will be restored, and we will bow to no one."

Answers echoed around the globe. Deep underground in New York City, in a lightless and abandoned inner sanctum, a faint tapping began.

It was coming from inside the painted stone of a false door, with only rats to hear it. In a cemetery in London, a more insistent sound clawed the night. And elsewhere, the first faint stirrings of life, long delayed. Of evil, long dormant.

ABOUT THE AUTHOR

Michael Northrop has written short fiction for *Weird Tales*, the *Notre Dame Review*, and *McSweeney's*. His first young adult novel, *Gentlemen*, earned him a *Publishers Weekly* Flying Start citation for a notable debut, and his second, *Trapped*, was an Indie Next List selection. NPR picked Michael's middle-grade novel *Plunked* for their Backseat Book Club. He has also written about a rescued Rottweiler in *Rotten* and, most recently, some treacherous seas in *Surrounded By Sharks*. An editor at *Sports Illustrated Kids* for many years, Michael now writes full-time from his home in New York City. Visit him online at www.michaelnorthrop.net.

READ THE FIRST CHAPTER
OF THE NEXT ADVENTURE

TOMBQUEST

AMULET KEEPERS

A downpour of red rain. Missing children across London. All signs point to another Death Walker on the prowl.

Alex and Ren's quest takes them to London's darkest corners – but will they be in time to stop the Death Walker?

Each book unlocks traps and treasure in the TombQuest game!

LOG IN NOW TO JOIN THE ADVENTURE.
scholastic.com/tombquest

DEAD MAN WALKING

A large figure descended the steep slope of Swain's Lane in north London. The man's features were old, but his frame was strong and he moved in long, sure strides. Each step of his heavy, old boots brought him closer to the slumbering neighbourhood below. The warm summer night was dark out here so far from the city's glittering centre. The man brushed one heavy hand against the tall black fence posts as he passed.

Thick fingernails struck old iron: *Tik tik tik*!

On the other side lay a very old cemetery, built into the hillside. He looked in at the moss-shrouded grounds with ink-dark eyes: considering, remembering. The cemetery was mostly full now, had been since World War I. It was a sleepy place. Deathly quiet. *Tik tik tik*! He let his hand drop. The fence ended; the village began.

The man moved more quietly now, like a cat settling in for the hunt. The first little houses appeared, huddled close together, their windows dark. A few moments later, he saw light up ahead, movement. The faintest hint of a smile formed on his death-parched lips.

"Aw, don't eat that!" said Bennie Kemp, tugging on the leash. "Spitfire! Spitfire! Bad dog!"

The British bulldog looked back and, reluctantly, dropped the candy wrapper. *Empty anyway*, his little dog brain thought.

"Just do your business and let's go," said his owner. "Creepy out here."

Spitfire looked back blankly. He understood several words – food, walk, biscuit – but none of those.

Bennie looked around the streets of his little

neighbourhood. He was surprised how deserted they were. He'd heard the rumours, of course. Everyone had. But having been raised on tales of British daring-do, he was a little disappointed in his neighbours. *A few people go missing and the whole town shuts down*, he thought. He could barely manage half a thought for the reports of blood falling from the sky and other mysterious events. He chalked that all up to public hysteria stoked by the media.

"Bunch o' nonsense," he said grouchily to Spitfire's back.

The dog didn't even bother to turn around this time. Talk to me when you've got a biscuit. Instead, he kept feverishly sniffing the ground with his blunt, slobber-covered snout. There was something dead up ahead, and he Had To Find It! Now he was the one tugging on the leash. It could be anything: a squirrel, a pigeon, a cat – oh, how he hoped it was a cat! He pulled his owner towards the smell.

As Bennie followed his lumpy little leader out of the glow of one street light and towards the glow of another, he saw a man. *It is a man, isn't it*? he thought. His face was creased with deep lines, but his body was large and solid. The combination reminded Bennie of a statue from a village green. The outfit, too. He looked like an explorer from the height of Britain's colonial might. *Dressed for the heat of India or Africa*, Bennie thought.

"You all right, then?" said Bennie. "Gave me a fright."

Spitfire finally peeled his stubby nose from the sidewalk. *Well, this was the dead thing*, he thought. *But it's all wrong.*

The man released a slow, ragged breath – air moving through damaged passageways like the hiss of old pipes – and then he looked up. Bennie got a better look at the man's skin now. Even in the faint light, he could see that it was horribly uneven, too leathery in some places, too loose in others. And then he saw the eyes.

Oh dear Lord, the eyes . . .

A scream pierced the night, followed by a few quick, sharp barks. One final yelp and the streets were silent again. And all around them, the houses were quiet, too. A bedside lamp clicked on and then quickly clicked off again. The rest of the windows remained dark. The neighbours stayed in their beds, pulling the sheets a little closer.

And so none of them saw the powerful figure of one man drag the limp frame of another out of the light at the edge of the village and up the long rise of Swain's Lane.

The rest of the night crept by without incident. Heavy eyes closed again, troubled minds found a few hours of rest, and a frightened bulldog huddled against a locked door. But the horrors were not quite over for the lonely dog's former owner.

Early the next morning, hidden from the freshly risen sun, an ancient ritual began. The residents woke from broken sleep and bad dreams to the sound of rain thumping off their roofs, spattering against their windowpanes. If there's one thing the English know, it's the sound of rain. And these drops were too thick, by the sound of them, to be mere water.

TQ